MW01135459

TEMPORARILY

Yours

A SHILLINGS AGENCY NOVEL

TEMPORARILY

 Yours

A SHILLINGS AGENCY NOVEL

DIANE ALBERTS

This book is a work of fiction. Names, characters, places, and incidents
are the product of the author's imagination or are used fictitiously.
Any resemblance to actual events, locales, or persons, living or dead, is
coincidental.

Copyright © 2014 by Diane Alberts. All rights reserved, including the
right to reproduce, distribute, or transmit in any form or by any means.
For information regarding subsidiary rights, please contact the Publisher.

Entangled Publishing, LLC
2614 South Timberline Road
Suite 109
Fort Collins, CO 80525
Visit our website at www.entangledpublishing.com.

Brazen is an imprint of Entangled Publishing, LLC. For more
information on our titles, visit www.brazenbooks.com.

Edited by Shannon Godwin
Cover design by Heather Howland

Manufactured in the United States of America

First Edition February 2014

This one is for my mom. Thank you, and I love you.

Chapter One

Cooper eyed the crowded airport with all of the excitement of a prisoner looking at his solitary confinement cell. Festive red, green, and white shades of the holiday season surrounded him, and every single boarding area looked identical to the next. Then again, didn't they always? Crying kids, harrowed mothers, fathers on their phones, and kids playing with their Christmas toys filled almost every single chair.

Weren't people supposed to stop dressing like it was Christmas after the twenty-sixth? Or maybe it was his inescapable Scrooge-iness making him feel that way. He hadn't been merry on Christmas, and he hadn't been happy on New Year's, either.

He hadn't been happy in a long damn time.

He rubbed his eyes and scanned the seating area. There was one empty chair left, next to a gorgeous brown haired woman in a red turtleneck sweater, matching heels, and a black knee-length skirt. With a face and legs like those, she was probably saving the seat for her husband—some lucky bastard who probably didn't appreciate her as he should.

She looked up at him, as if she sensed his scrutiny, but quickly looked back down at her iPhone. The contact was brief, but even so, he saw the flare of appreciation in those bright blue eyes as she dropped her head.

She liked what she saw—missing husband or no.

He approached her, his focus locked on her the whole time. He stopped when he got close enough to speak without calling across the room, opened his mouth, and then—

"Hey, Mister. You're on my coat."

Just as Cooper turned to apologize to the child speaking, the kid slammed a candy cane into Cooper's stomach—pointy end first. Another kid pulled the jacket out from under Cooper's feet, and he stumbled backward. He hit the floor so hard his breath whooshed out of him in a painful wheeze. His face was turned toward the gate, where the attendant gaped at him, and a red heel rested on the floor beside his head.

Damn it, he recognized those heels.

"Are you okay?" the woman asked. Though her question was one expressing concern, he couldn't help but hear the amusement in there, too. "Do you need help getting up?"

Turning his head, he followed the line of her knockout legs, all the way up until he could see her angelic face, framed by the most touchable brown hair he'd ever seen. He would *not* look any lower. If not for the way she held her knees together, he would be getting arrested for being a peeping tom, for Christ's sake.

He was literally in between her legs, his head halfway under her chair.

Still seated, she bent over him awkwardly, looking down at him with a wrinkled brow and shining blue eyes. Though he had been fantasizing about her legs, he hadn't exactly wanted to get close to them in *this* way.

Cursing under his breath, he scooted down and away from her on his back, feeling a bit like an overturned turtle, then rolled to his feet as gracefully as he could manage under the circumstances. Smoothing his jacket over his arms, he ducked his head to hide his hot cheeks. "No, I'm fine. Thank you."

As he straightened the collar of his jacket, he eyed the fair-skinned beauty. The concern was gone, and she was doing a poor job of hiding a smile behind her hand. Hell, he even saw a dimple.

She pointed to his stomach. The candy cane that the child had speared him with hung from his brand new cashmere sweater—with the help of a coating of saliva and sugar.

"I'm so sorry!" the horrified mother said, grabbing her son and pushing him behind her body for protection, as if she was worried Cooper might attack. "I think he's been watching too many superhero movies."

"Are you saying I look like a villain?" he asked with a smile on his face, trying to set the woman at ease. When the mother opened her mouth to reply, he shook his head and patted her arm. "No harm done. Really." With two fingers, Cooper removed the sticky weapon from his sweater and handed it over. "Don't worry about it."

The mother smiled with gratitude and took the gooey mess without flinching. "Thank you for being so understanding."

"You're welcome."

Once he turned his back to her, he let the smile fade away. Eyeing his sticky fingers in disgust, he looked for the nearest water fountain. He didn't want to wander too far and risk the chance of missing takeoff. He already knew there wouldn't be another open flight to North Carolina with an available seat until tomorrow night at ten, and he needed to be on this one.

Sure, he didn't *have* to leave *this* early. He could've easily pushed his departure back a few days. He didn't have to report for his new job until next week. But he needed to escape his father's incessant pressure. He didn't approve of Cooper going back overseas. He felt Cooper should stay continental and work for him at the company he had formed specifically for military dropouts.

Dropouts like Cooper.

Yeah. Thanks, but no thanks.

"Would you like a Wet One?" a musical voice asked, tickling over his senses and ripping him from his thoughts. Without even looking, he knew who had spoken. It was the woman in the turtleneck whom he'd practically landed on… or *under*, rather.

"A wet what?" He turned slowly, his brow raised. She was holding what looked like a baby wipe in her right hand and a container in her left. He couldn't help but notice she didn't wear a wedding ring. So there was no husband? Smiling, he reached out and took the offered wipe. "Oh. Sure. Thank you. Is that seat taken?"

"No, you can have it." She gazed up at him, sending his heart rate through the roof, and then looked away. There was something about her that made him forget about everything that had been hanging over his head past year. And, man, he needed that right now. Scooting her long legs out of the way, she smiled and motioned him to sit. "That kid came out of nowhere, huh?"

"Like a ninja warrior," he agreed, getting comfortable on the chair. He quirked his lips at the amusement in her eyes. "Thanks for letting me know I still had the weapon stuck on my shirt."

She laughed. Damn, but she had an adorable laugh. "You're welcome."

"I was so worried about being late and missing this flight, I hadn't even figured getting attacked into the equation." He cleaned off his sweater with the wipe and dropped the Wet One into the trashcan next to him. If she carried those things around in her purse, one of these rug rats running around might be hers. "Thanks for the wipe, by the way. You carry them around for your children?"

"Oh, God, no. I don't even have a husband, let alone kids. If I were going to have kids, I would be married for at least two years beforehand. By then, people pass the mark where one in twelve marriages fail. I personally think they fall apart around then because that's when the attraction wears off, and the couple looks for that draw elsewhere. Bringing kids into the equation before that whole mess is foolish." She smoothed her curly brown hair and flushed, then hastily tucked a wayward strand behind her ear. "Not that you asked about my beliefs in the institute of marriage. I'm sorry. I know I'm babbling."

"Believe it or not, that was my next question," he said, grinning. "Tell me, how do you feel about the four-year mark? Is that a catastrophe, too?"

"Don't even get me started on what happens at four

years…if you even make it that far. Most of the time, they—" She broke off and gave a strangled laugh. "I'm sorry. You're clearly just asking these questions to be nice, or to humor me or whatever, and I'm answering in way too much detail. Like, way, *way* too much detail. I'm just nervous. Really, *really* nervous." She paused and cocked her head. "And now I'm repeating myself a good quarter of this conversation, too. Lovely. Just lovely."

He studied her with new curiosity. What she thought embarrassing, he found refreshing. Where did she find her statistics from, anyway? How the hell did she know that one in twelve marriages fail at the two-year mark?

Time to find out.

"Let me guess. Divorce lawyer? Marriage counselor?"

She scoffed. "Worse. I'm an actuary—quite possibly the most boring job to ever exist."

"You don't look boring to me," he said, his voice husky. He blinked. Wait, why did his voice change? What the fuck? "Quite the opposite."

She shot him a surprised look. "Are you flirting with me?"

Did she actually *ask* him if he was *flirting* with her? Fascinating. "And if I am?"

"Well, uh." Her cheeks flushed red and she fidgeted with her skirt. "Thanks, I guess? It's a welcome distraction, if nothing else."

Wow. That almost hurt. He bit the inside of his cheek to stop himself from smiling. She was just…so refreshingly *different*. "That's all? I must be losing my touch."

She tucked another loose curl behind her ear, as if trying to hide nervousness. "I wouldn't know, having just met you.

Plus, I'm hardly an expert, being an actuary."

He laughed. He hadn't had this much fun talking to a stranger in…well, ever. "Is there a rule that actuaries are bad judges of character?"

"No." She raised her brows. "We're quite excellent."

He gave her a once-over. "Hm. I'll have to reserve my judgment. Until I know a bit more about you anyway."

"Reserve away." She gave him another look, this one lingering a little longer. "I have to ask, do you know what an actuary is? I've never heard someone claim it's interesting in any way, shape, or form."

He pursed his lips. "I know it involves a hell of a lot of odd knowledge about percentages and random stats. And that I'm sitting next to one right now."

She grinned. "Close enough."

He ran his hand through his hair and she watched. When she licked her lips, he saw her pupils flare inside those baby blues. A responding heat flushed through him, making him want to scoot closer. "So…why are you nervous? Afraid a kid will attack you next?" He held a hand to his heart. "I swear to protect you from the ruffians at all costs."

She shook her head. Pointing out the window at their plane, she said, "I'm not worried about kids, but I am frightened of that deathtrap people continue to erroneously call an airplane. Airborne coffin is a more accurate description, if you ask me."

He eyed the plane before turning his attention back to her. "You're scared of flying?"

"Terrified." She closed her eyes and flopped back against the seat, growing paler before his eyes. "Horrified. Certain I'm going to die."

"Then why are you doing it?"

She peeked at him, her pretty mouth puckered up as if she waited for a kiss. Or maybe he'd imagined that last part. "You want the truth?"

"And nothing but the truth."

She chuckled. "I have to go to my sister's wedding, where I have to pretend I'm happy and perfectly okay with my fictional boyfriend's absence." She clamped a hand over her mouth and closed her eyes. "I didn't mean to add that last detail in. Ignore it."

He raised a brow. "Not a chance, sweetheart. Fictional, huh? I find that hard to believe."

"You'd be surprised," she muttered through her hand. Sighing, she dropped her hand and picked up her expensive looking purse. She held onto the straps so tightly he could make out the details of every single one of her knuckles. "I need to shut up now. I'm sorry. Again."

She really was nervous as hell about the flight. Cooper didn't think he'd ever seen anyone quite so jittery, and he'd seen a hell of a lot. "Don't apologize. You can tell me anything you want. And the best part is you'll never see me again, so you don't have to worry about facing me after. But tell me…why would someone as beautiful as you have to make up a boyfriend? You should have at least six at home waiting for you."

Real smooth there, Cooper.

"Yeah, well, I don't." She flushed an even deeper red and looked down at her lap. He got a brief glance of her nibbling on her deliciously pink lip before she ducked her head. "And I'm okay with that. I don't place much stock in the whole aspect of 'love saving all.' I'm not exactly the relationship type. I think they're largely a waste of time."

He hadn't been expecting to hear that from her. Most of the women he spent time with were of the loose variety, and they had the same beliefs as him when it came to relationships—as in they were a waste of time. But she hardly came across as *that* type of girl. She didn't seem the type to love 'em and leave 'em, so to speak. She was an enigma he longed to figure out. "Because of the dreaded two year mark?"

She shrugged. "Yeah. That and so much more."

He found himself wanting to argue with her. Why? He wasn't big on love and relationships, either. He hadn't found "the one" yet, and he was starting to think she didn't exist. And he was leaving the country, so he didn't have room in his life for a woman who would worry about him.

But still…

"Sometimes, it's possible, despite the odds. Just look at me, for example."

She looked up at him in surprise. Hell, he was surprised he was debating statistics and the probability of love with her, too.

"Statistically speaking," he continued, "the odds of being stabbed in the stomach with a candy cane are one in three point six million…yet here I am with a ruined sweater."

"You made that statistic up," she said, her eyes shining.

"I did," he admitted. "But I'm pretty sure I'm close to accurate on my figures."

"That's true," she agreed, her lips turning up at the corners. "I certainly haven't heard of that happening to anyone before."

He nodded and nudged her with his shoulder. "See?

Statistics aren't everything. I'm Cooper Shillings, by the way."

"Kayla. Kayla Moriarity." She held her hand out, and he shook it, his fingers gently brushing her wrist. She uncrossed her legs and re-crossed them, and then pulled away. "Nice to meet you, Cooper."

Damn. The sound of her saying his name was pure magic.

The speaker crackled and a feminine voice announced, "Attention passengers, we are now boarding first class for Flight 342. First class only, please."

"Oh, God." Kayla took a deep breath and stood. "Oh, God. Oh, God. Here we g-go. Are you first class, too?"

He repressed a snort. First class his ass. "'Fraid not."

"That's too bad. I could have used some more distracting… or was it flirting?"

He grinned. "You'll never know now."

"One of life's unanswered mysteries, I suppose." She looked at him one last time, then hiked her purse onto her shoulder. "Hey, thanks for talking to me. It helped take my mind off things. If we somehow manage to walk away from this alive, I'll say hello to you at baggage claim."

He never travelled with more than a small carry-on suitcase—something else his overbearing father drilled into his head at a young age—but he'd go to the baggage claim anyway to check on her. Maybe he shouldn't care so much how a stranger fared through a flight, and yet…he did. "You'll be fine. I'll see you later."

Her expression showed her doubt at his words, but instead of arguing about it, she headed for the desk with nothing but a purse on her shoulder and a ticket on her hand. He watched her walk away, ignoring the sick feeling of inadequacy in his gut. He swallowed hard, wishing he'd shelled out the extra bucks for a first class seat.

The way she spouted out statistics and percentages combined with the elegant way she held herself showed him she was well-off and educated. She'd probably been born with a silver spoon in her mouth and a Tiffany rattle in her hand.

She wouldn't know what to do with a wounded warrior, so it was probably for the best that he wasn't going to have the chance to talk to her again. He was a failure who couldn't be counted on to… Well, to do anything.

Only two other people followed her. That meant there had to be at least one seat open in first class. Maybe more. He tapped his fingers on his knee, cursing under his breath. She might be sitting all alone on the plane. There would be no one to babble at when she was nervous. No one to calm her nerves, or make her forget about her fears.

Worried. Scared. Alone.

Damn it. She'd awoken his deeply-repressed urge to protect anyone who needed help, and he couldn't get the voice in the back of his head to shut the hell up. As she disappeared into the jet bridge, Cooper stood and stalked to the desk. "Excuse me, but is it too late to change my ticket to first class? If it's available, I'd like the seat directly next to Ms. Moriarity, please."

The woman at the desk scowled. "We're boarding, sir. We don't normally allow changes this close to the flight."

Cooper smiled his most charming smile. "I understand ma'am, but my friend who just boarded is scared to death. I think the flight will go a lot more smoothly for her—and for the flight attendants—if I can sit next to her." He shrugged.

"You know how jumpy passengers can be."

She looked at him for a moment and sighed. "Yes, unfortunately, I do." After punching a few keys on her keyboard, her attention on the screen in front of her, she said, "I can make it happen, but it'll be three hundred dollars more, sir."

He pictured his almost empty bank account, but ignored the voice of common sense shouting at him to sit the hell back down. Pulling out his credit card, he slid it across the desk.

Kayla needed someone to distract her from her fears.

She needed him.

Chapter Two

Kayla settled into in her window seat, pulled the tray down, and swiped a Wet One over it. She wasn't a certified germaphobe or anything, but lots of disgusting things crossed airplane trays. From snotty hands to spilled food... and beyond. How many people had joined the mile high club on this very plane?

She shuddered just thinking about it.

Once she finished cleaning, she got her emergency flight stuff in order. The flight might only be a few hours long, but she'd be spending it with her eyes shut to the world. Sleeping mask? Check. Sleeping pills? Check. Now all she needed was one of those cocktails they offered in first class—she'd already ordered a vodka cranberry—and she'd be done for the night.

When she woke up, she'd be back in North Carolina with her parents, and the real fun could start.

Yeah. Not really.

Every time she saw them, they harped on her. Asked why she hadn't settled down yet. She'd argue with them, telling them she was young and single and free. And they would proceed to ignore her explanations for her life choices. They did it every visit. It never varied.

But this visit wasn't going to be the same old scenario.

Hence the fake boyfriend.

A gear kicked into place, or a door shut somewhere, and she jumped. Though Cooper had managed to keep her distracted in the boarding area, nothing could stop her from panicking now. Although the image of him getting gutted with a candy cane *did* bring a smile to her face. And, holy hell, the man was hot…even with a sticky sweater.

Those green eyes, paired with that light brown hair that had curled just right at the ends, had been a hell of a welcome distraction. And his lips…man, they'd been so sensual and full. It had made her wonder if he was a good kisser.

If he sat next to her on this flight, she might not even care that they were thousands and thousands of feet up in the air with nothing to save them when their deathtrap crashed to the earth below. Maybe she'd even discover if those lips were as kissable as they looked.

Okay. Enough of that line of thought. She didn't even know the guy. It was probably a good thing he wasn't sitting next to her. If he was, she wouldn't be able to pass out through the flight until safely back on the ground again.

Because if she slept, she might snore. Or worse…drool all over his shoulder.

That would be an unforgiveable offense.

The flight attendant walked up to her with the double vodka cranberry she'd requested the second she'd boarded the plane, and Kayla was grateful that being in first class meant the drinks were mixed for her. Her hands were shaking so badly there was no way she could have done it herself.

"Thank you." With jerky movements, she lifted the glass to her lips and gulped down three big swallows. "I needed this."

Come on liquid courage.

If the flight attendant was shocked by Kayla's desperate display, she didn't show it. "Can I get you anything else, or would you like some peace and quiet now?"

Kayla eyed the passengers in front of her. Hopefully they wouldn't be too noisy. "Quiet is good. I plan on passing out shortly so I'm not alive as we crash down to our fiery deaths," Kayla blurted, her heart racing and her mouth drying out while her hands inexplicably got all sweaty. Trembling, she set her cocktail into the drink holder next to her seat. "I'm scared of flying. Really scared."

The flight attendant blinked at her. "Don't worry. We have one of the best pilots flying us today. You don't have a thing to worry about."

"Does he drink? Or do drugs?"

She laughed. "No. They're pretty strict about that stuff nowadays."

"I hope you're right."

The flight attendant smiled one more time, then backed off. "I'm going to check on the others now."

Kayla bit her lip and watched the attendant leave. The woman probably thought she was one brick short of a house. Well, she could think what she wanted as long as she kept the drinks coming. Kayla put the sleeping pills on the travel table, thankful she didn't have to worry about driving once she landed. After her self-medication, she'd be in no shape to operate heavy machinery.

Or to talk about *any*thing, really…which was why she would be taking a shuttle to the hotel. Once there, she would spend a peaceful night alone, catching as much sleep as she could before the insanity of the wedding preparations consumed her.

She muttered, "I'm going to toss back this drink. Then off to sleep I go."

Soft laughter sounded beside her, and she stiffened. "You're adorable when you talk to yourself. You know that? But you don't have to anymore. You've got me."

"Cooper?" She blinked up at him, trying to put two and two together. "You're in first class, too? But you said you weren't."

"I thought wrong. My, uh, travel agent told me I had to fly coach, but when I saw first class wasn't booked, I switched." He rubbed the back of his neck and shuffled his feet. "Your purse is in my seat."

"Oh." Swallowing hard, she moved it over so he could sit next to her. Snatching up the sleeping pills, she tossed them in her purse before he noticed—no way would she be taking them now—and threw the dirty wipe in with them. "Sorry about that. I forgot I'd have company."

"It sure looks like you planned for company," he said, with a pointed look at the nearly-clear-it-was-so-strong drink next to her. God, his eyes were so freaking green she couldn't help but wonder if they were contacts. No one had eyes that color naturally. "Drinking to get rid of the nerves?"

Hell yeah.

She lifted the glass and tried to sip demurely, but she was pretty sure it sounded like a loud slurp instead. "It won't get rid of them, but it will make them a little more bearable. I apologize in advance for any drunken rambling I'm about to make. Though it probably won't sound much different from my nervous babbling."

God, she needed to stop sounding like a fool.

If they'd met under any other circumstances, she would have remained cool and collected the whole time. Flirted with all of the ease and confidence she could muster.

Instead, he got this.

Luckily, he didn't seem to mind the half-wit state she was currently stuck in. Grinning, he shoved his bag in the overhead. As he reached up, his sweater lifted, showing off his taut abdomen peppered with the same color light brown hair that was on his head. Only this time, the hair led down below his beltline to his...

Never mind where it led, thank you very much. She curled her hands into fists at the ridiculous urge to touch the thin strip of skin.

"If you're going to have a party, the least I can do is join you." He looked over his shoulder at the attendant who hovered in the corner. "Excuse me? Could I please have what she's having?"

"Of course," she said, the appreciation for the fine male specimen in front of her clear in the attendant's enraptured expression. This was not lost on Kayla. Miraculously enough, Cooper didn't seem to notice, though. "I'll be right back with that."

"Thank you."

As the attendant hurried off to make his drink, Cooper

sat beside Kayla, dragged a hand through his hair and turned those bright green eyes her way. When he looked at her like that, all concerned and warm, her insides went all gooey and hot. She wondered if he knew the effect he had on her.

Not if she could help it. She lifted her chin and clenched her teeth together, flashing him a smile. She would *not* lose herself in him like some foolish besotted schoolgirl. "So…?"

"So…?" He smiled back, those lips she was so obsessed with parting to show his perfect white teeth. The man was flawless everywhere. *So* not fair. "Are you topping this drink off with some sleeping pills? I saw you had something out earlier."

Crap. She hadn't moved fast enough. "Uh, no. They were vitamins."

He cocked a brow. "Vitamins? On a plane?"

"Yeah. Haven't you heard of them before?" she teased, tugging on a piece of hair and looking at him through her lashes. "They're good for you—unlike the vodka I'm about to down. I figured I'd balance out the bad effects of the alcohol on my liver with something good. Life is all about ratios, after all."

The attendant brought him his drink but he didn't tear his eyes from Kayla. Having his full attention made her tremble. She looked out the window, needing a respite from…well, *him*.

The attendant set the drink down—along with a refill for Kayla, bless her heart—and cleared her throat. "Here you go. If you need anything else, just press the call button."

"Could you bring us a blanket? Besides that, we should be fine," Cooper said. After the attendant left, he shifted closer to Kayla until his leg pressed against hers. Then, with his voice low and his gaze locked on her mouth, he said, "You looked cold."

The shudder? Yeah. That hadn't been from the cold. But let him think it was. "Yeah, a little."

"I'll do my best to distract you from the flight," he promised, taking a sip of his drink. "You know that, right?"

She furrowed her brow. "Why do you want to? You don't even know me. What's in it for you?"

"Does there have to be something in it for me?"

"There usually is." She met his eyes. They looked as kind and open as they had earlier. Was it all an act or what? "Most of the time, anyway. What's your play?"

He shrugged. "I like you. I like talking to you. That's about it."

"And now you want to sit with me and make me happy?" She crossed her arms. "It sounds like you're trying to fill the role of my make-believe boyfriend for the next couple of hours."

"Yeah, maybe something like that." He reached for the vodka cranberry and his woodsy scent teased her senses. "I find you intriguing and I enjoy your company. Isn't that enough of a reason to try to help you? To talk to you?"

"I guess." She watched him closely, taking in all his perfection with the eye of a cynic. Guys that looked like him usually weren't the selfless type. That might be stereotyping a bit, sure, but it was *true*. "And yet, not really."

His gaze fell to her lips. She could practically feel his mouth on hers already, kissing her until she forgot all about her fears. This was bad. Really bad. He might be here out of the kindness of his heart, but her body was far too drawn to him.

How long had it been since she wanted a man? Months? Years?

As if he could read her thoughts, he leaned closer. "I still don't see how someone like you would have to make up a boyfriend. How is that possible?"

"I told you." Her pulse increased. "I haven't met anyone worth the trouble of a relationship yet. I'm picky when it comes to men."

"Hm. Maybe you're looking in the wrong places." He reached out and touched her hand, his fingers light on her skin. She knew she should pull away, but instead her gaze clashed with his and she didn't move. "Have you ever thought of that?"

Oh, so he was playing that game, was he? All right, she could flirt with him too. Maybe it would even take her mind off of her flying fears. He'd certainly helped in the terminal before the flight boarded. She looked up at him through her lashes, leaning in *just* right. "Or maybe the man for me has been hanging around in airports all this time."

The corners of his mouth tilted up. "Perhaps."

She tapped her fingers on her thigh, inwardly rejoicing at his reaction to her. "So, you're all mine tonight?"

"*All* yours," he repeated, smiling wolfishly at her. "However you'd like me."

The attendant came back, carrying a plastic package with a blanket in it. Cooper accepted it, thanking her quietly, and Kayla just watched him.

Why did his words sound so naughty? Maybe he'd meant them that way. Or maybe she just wanted him to have meant them that way. The words were innocent enough, yet desire spiraled in her stomach. There was something about

Cooper...

She *liked* him.

Picking up her almost empty glass, she held it out for a toast. "To vodka and not dying?"

"Especially to the not dying part." He clanked his cup against hers. "You know, I have a very effective way to make you forget your fear that I would love to show you—if you're willing to trust me, that is."

She swayed closer. "Oh? And what would that be?"

He shifted in his seat, closing the distance between them until his lips were a breath away from her cheek. He tucked her hair behind her ear, and she shivered at the light touch. "*Distraction*. I'm going to make you forget all about how high we are in the sky. By the time we land, you'll be sad to see the flight end because you'll have to say goodbye to me."

Such confidence...but damn if she didn't think he was right.

"Oh, really?" Swallowing hard, she said, "How do you propose to do something as impossible as that? You did hear the part about me being super picky, right?"

"Oh, I heard you all right." He settled back into his seat. "As far as how I plan to distract you? Well, that, my dear, is for me to know and you to find out. But first, we drink."

She chugged back her drink, her heart racing the whole time. Only, instead of fear of flying being the guilty culprit, it was the man sitting next to her. Damn, he was good. They both set down their empty glasses, and she shuddered. "God, that's strong. I should've asked for more juice."

His lips twitched, and he trailed a finger down her jawline. "Know what chases a strong drink better than the cranberry juice?"

The contact of his hand on her face sent shivers of lust through her blood, making her feel weak and dizzy. Or maybe it was the strong cocktail she just drank as if it were water instead of almost straight booze. Or perhaps it was because she had no idea what he'd do next—and liked that about him.

Oh, the hell with it. She pressed her face into his palm, relishing the touch instead of ending it. "No. What chases a strong drink better than cranberry juice?"

"This."

Before she could so much as blink, his lips were on hers, and the harsh taste of vodka was replaced with his mouth. Those lips she'd been fantasizing about closed over hers, taking the breath right out of her. She gasped at his unexpected move, and he took full advantage of her surprise.

When his tongue swept inside and touched hers, she moaned. Actually *moaned.*

She should have been shoving him off, but instead she pulled him closer. Dear God, the man knew what he was doing. It had been a long time since she'd been kissed…or anything else, for that matter. And he was fabulous.

Groaning, he tilted his head so he could have better access to her mouth, held her face still with his hand, and proceeded to ravish her. There couldn't possibly be another word for what he did. No doubt. No hesitation. He assumed he was welcome to seduce her…a stranger he'd met moments ago in an *airport.*

And, damn it, she wanted more than a kiss. She wanted it all, God help her.

She'd never been so turned on by something so simple before. She clenched her thighs together, desire dampening her panties. She rubbed against the seat and slid her tongue into his mouth, flicking it against his. Pulling back slightly, he took a deep breath and rubbed a thumb down her lip. "You taste even better than I thought you would."

Then he reached across her. His knuckles brushed against her lap as he tightened her seatbelt strap, perilously close to where she ached for him to touch. Teasing her, scandalizing her, before settling in his own seat as if nothing had happened.

What. The. Hell?

The flight attendant approached them, a pleasant expression on her face. Kayla searched for any signs of awareness that her two passengers just had their tongues in one another's mouths, but saw nothing. "I'll collect your drinks, and you'll need to put your trays up. We're about to take off."

"Of course." His voice even, he handed off his empty glass with a steady hand and then grabbed Kayla's as well. "Once we're in the air, we'd like another round—but a quarter of the strength."

"Certainly."

She headed off. When he turned to Kayla and looked at her with the unmistakable intention to reenact the make-out session from a few moments ago, she blurted out the first thing that came to mind. "Are you trying to get me drunk so you can kiss me again?"

"Perhaps." His lips quirked up a little bit. "Though, a more accurate description of what I'm trying to accomplish would be to get you drunk enough to forget about the flight, but not so drunk that I'm stuck cleaning vomit off my shoes. It's a thin line I'm walking here."

"You might have to clean it up anyway," she muttered, looking out the window. Clinging to the armrests as if they would possibly save her in a crash, she closed her eyes. "Oh, God, we're moving. Aren't they supposed to do that stupid drill about floating aircraft seats and escaping out the emergency door to die in the ocean *before* we take off?"

"She's about to start. See? Besides, we're just getting in line on the tarmac."

The attendant started her spiel about what to do in case of a crash, and it took all of Kayla's control not to laugh hysterically. As if they stood a chance if they crashed.

Puh-lease.

The aircraft turned onto the runway, and she grabbed the armrest tighter. "Oh. God."

The flight attendant stopped talking and went to sit down. She looked so calm. *How* could she be so freaking calm at a time like this?

"I'm here." He grabbed her hand and pulled it into his lap, right above his knee. Instead of pulling away, she held on tight. As if he could keep her safe or something. "I'll keep you safe."

And he'd read her mind *again*. "Oh really?" She opened her eyes so she could glower at him. "Are you really Superman in disguise? You're going to catch the plane as it plummets to the earth?"

He snapped the fingers of his free hand. "Yep. You figured out my secret. Underneath my sweater, I'm hiding spandex and a cape."

"That's kind of hot." She pictured him in the Superman outfit, tight fabric hugging every muscle. "Okay, really hot."

He snorted and squeezed her hand. "Talk to me. I'll

distract you as we climb."

She let out a half-groan, half-laugh and looked out the window. Though they were only taxiing down the runway, they might as well have been going three hundred miles an hour from what she could see. "I heard once that almost all plane crashes occur on takeoff or landing, but they rarely occur in mid-flight."

"Actually, only fourteen percent of accidents occur during takeoff. Fifty-seven percent happen while up in the air," he said. "It's a myth that takeoff is the most dangerous part. I know that for a fact."

"What?" She shot him a surprised look. "Don't tell me. Are you an actuary, too?"

He shook his head. "Nope. I'm an ex-Marine, currently on my way to my new job."

"Oh." She relaxed a little bit. "Okay. That makes me feel a little safer. I've always had a thing for a man in uniform."

"Good." He stroked his thumb over her knuckles. "I've always had a thing for pretty little actuaries."

Her heart skipped a beat even though it was so clearly a pickup line. But he'd called her *pretty*. Her inner schoolgirl was totally *squee-ing* all over the place right now. "Have you ever met an actuary before me?"

"Nope." He grinned. "But I don't need to."

"Is that so?"

"Mmhm. I now know I always had a thing for them. Especially ones who wear skirts and taste like heaven." He leaned closer and brushed a soft kiss against her lips again. She barely had time to react before he pulled back, making a sound deep in his throat that was more erotic than she could ever explain. "Yep. Definitely heaven."

The urge to fan her cheeks was strong. She needed to cool it right now. This man was *way* too good.

As they started to gain altitude, she clung to his hand and scrambled for something to talk about besides kissing. "Oh, God. Distraction. Distraction is good. You said ex, right? So, you're out of the Marines? Were you in for four years? Did you know thirty-nine percent of new recruits quit after the initial four years?"

"No, I didn't." He laughed. "Buy, yep, I got out after four years. Now I'll be working for a private sector security company that's going back to Afghanistan into enemy territory next week. I start Monday."

"It's sending you overseas?"

"Yep."

Oh, great. So her mysterious benefactor would be gone from the country after this weekend. For some reason that didn't sit well. "Well, I wish you good luck. Where do you live when you're not rescuing women in airports?"

"I'm from Maine." He kissed the back of her hand. "But the company I work for is in North Carolina, so I guess I'll be spending most of my free time there. How about you?"

"I'm the opposite. I grew up near Charlotte but I live in Maine." Shivering, she shifted closer to him. She knew he was only touching and kissing her to make her forget about the flight, but if he kept that up, she'd be climbing in his lap before it was over. "I live in Cape Elizabeth, to be exact."

He turned her hand over and nibbled on her wrist. "My parents live there, too."

"Mm," she murmured, not really listening.

He flicked his tongue over her palm this time, his gaze on her the whole time. She watched, mesmerized, as he nibbled at the spot he just licked. Even though she should pull away—she didn't.

"You taste delicious."

"You look delicious," she blurted, and then wished she hadn't. "I mean, uh…never mind."

Apparently, he didn't find her ridiculous at all. He smiled at her and moved his lips to her wrist. Pressing another soft kiss there, he looked up at her through his eyelashes— incredibly thick, long eyelashes that could make a woman weep with jealousy. "Here come our drinks."

"Wh-what?" She blinked and shook her head to clear the hazy fog of desire. "What did you say?"

He raised a brow. "I said our drinks are coming."

"It's been long enough for that? That's not possible." She turned towards the window. There was dark sky and… clouds. Freaking *clouds*. Not a city light to be seen. "But that's not possible."

"I assure you, it's quite possible."

Her jaw dropped. "How did I miss ten minutes like that?"

With a smug grin, he shrugged. "Distraction."

Oh, God, he was really, *really* good.

Chapter Three

Cooper looked away from Kayla and took a steadying breath. He had the suspicion she wasn't the type to kiss strangers on a plane, and yet she was letting him touch her. Kiss her. And he wanted more. So much more.

He hadn't boarded the plane with the intention of getting her into his bed, but now that he was here, he couldn't stop thinking about it. Her lips were sweeter than any he had ever tasted, and everything she did increased his desire. She gaped out the window in shock, but she might as well have been stripping naked for him. The hard-on he was sporting seemed to think she was, anyway.

This was the most fun he'd had in months. Hell, he didn't think he even remembered what the word *fun* meant. Not since he watched his best friend get killed in front of him. And not since he'd been forced to watch the woman Josh left behind fall apart—so much so that Cooper doubted she'd ever be the same again. How could she be?

Which was why he'd *never* put a woman through that shit.

It was why he would be single until he'd fulfilled his duties.

The flight attendant approached and smiled at him, setting down their drinks. After she left, he took a sip to make sure it was less strong than the previous round. He didn't want Kayla passing out on him. Satisfied, he placed the drink back on his tray.

"So, tell me about this boyfriend you made up for the benefit of your family. What does he do?"

"I'm still trying to decide between a doctor and a lawyer." She let out a huffy breath and looked up at the unlit seatbelt sign. "I'm not the best liar in the world, so I kind of keep putting the planning stage off."

"So they didn't grill you about him? It's weird considering they've been jonesing for you to find a man."

"Of course they grilled me. Or tried to, anyway. I fed them some lame line about wanting them to be surprised by everything about him when they met him and then made sure I had to get off the phone, like, immediately. Besides," a flush crept into her cheeks. "I didn't mean to lie. I kind of just blurted out the boyfriend story to get them off my back. It came out before I had time to think about it. And once it was out there…"

"You couldn't take it back."

She nodded. "I've been dodging questions ever since. I'm sure they suspect the truth but I'm not backing down."

"So all they know is that you have a boyfriend and he can't come home with you for your sister's wedding?"

"Right. But we supposedly spent Christmas and New

Year's Eve together at his family's house. And, of course, they wanted to speak to him to wish him a Merry Christmas. I'm still not sure how I managed to convince them that he was helping his mother with something."

He pictured her all alone for the holiday—all for the sake of perpetuating a lie. "Dump him. If he's too busy to go to your sister's wedding with you, then he shouldn't be your boyfriend."

"I can't *dump* him. He's not real."

He picked up her cocktail and passed it to her, his fingers brushing across her knuckles when she accepted the drink. He wanted to grab her hand and hold it in his, but held back so he didn't come on too strong. Touching her felt too damn good. "If I was your boyfriend, then you damn well wouldn't be sitting here alone on a plane with a stranger like me."

"He's not real, remember?" She took a small sip and wrinkled her brow. "Wow. I can taste the cranberry juice in this one."

Her comment made him laugh. "Is it a long distance relationship? That would explain why your man couldn't come to the wedding."

She rolled her eyes. "You might as well call it 'dead but don't know it yet' relationships. They never work."

He agreed with her views in this instance, but he couldn't resist teasing her. "Do you have the numbers to back that up?"

"Not exact statistics," she peeked at him, her lips curling up. "But I think it's pretty safe to say that four out of five of them fail."

He flinched. "Ouch. Though, I agree. I've seen it happen." He pointed at her. "But you need a good reason for boyfriend not to come along—or he'll look like a loser."

She tapped her fingers on her leg. "You might have a point. If he's supposed to be as wonderful as Susan's fiancé, why can't he come with me to the wedding? Hmmm... Maybe he needs to work."

"When is the wedding again?"

"Saturday, and Susan is my *younger* sister. She is marrying the perfect boy she dated in her perfect senior year of high school, the only man she ever slept with, blah, blah, blah." She waved her hands in a circle, then rolled her eyes. "You get the point."

"Sounds like she's perfect," he quipped.

"Yeah, pretty much." She grinned, then took another sip. Watching her pink lips, he'd never been so fucking jealous of a cup before. "And then there's me, with no one special in my life. No one I've ever been serious about, anyway. Just flings. But my family doesn't want to hear that. They want weddings and love and security."

"So you made him up to get them off your back?"

"Exactly. I'm the shame of the Moriarity family. It may seem a bit old-fashioned, but they think a woman of a certain age needs to be married with kids. The fact that I don't have a boyfriend, and—*gasp!*—my younger sister is getting married before me...well, let's just say it's code orange for my parents. It's a bit melodramatic, but there it is. I made up a boyfriend just so they don't worry about me. In all reality, I don't even want one. But if they knew that, they'd have it in their head that I'm miserable up in Maine all by myself."

Oh, he knew how that went. He was also one of the only ones in his family who wasn't seeing anyone. His mother was constantly suggesting nice women she knew. He lifted his glass to Kayla and took a drink. "I'm right there with you on the lack of relationships thing. A few months ago, my mother went so far as to chase down a woman in a parking lot to get her phone number for her 'hero son fighting overseas.'"

Kayla choked on a snort. "You're making that up."

"I wish I was," he said solemnly. "But it's a true story. One among many I could bore you with the whole flight."

She burst into uncontrollable laughter, clutching her stomach. He had a feeling the drink had more to do with her amusement than him, but he'd take it. She was intoxicating when she laughed. After she recovered, she swiped a tear away from the corner of her eye. "Oh my God, I would literally *pay* to see that. I'm not even kidding."

Truth be told, he would've too. His mother could be downright formidable when she was set on a goal, even if she wasn't even five feet tall. "If Mom was here with us right now, she'd be whispering little tidbits of information about me into your ear that would make you more inclined to make an honest man of me. Like one of those little angels on your shoulder you see in movies, only much more devious."

"Ooh, do tell." She unbuckled her seatbelt and turned to him, with her legs tucked under her. "What would she say to me?"

Her skirt hiked up, teasing him. His fingers itched to trace the hem and inch it a little bit higher on her thigh. Just an inch higher...

He pressed his lips together and shook his head, more at himself than at her question. He opened the package with the blanket and threw it over them. If nothing else, it would hide her tempting legs from his view. "No way. We're talking about you and your penchant for fake boyfriends. Not *me*."

She smoothed the blanket over their legs, pouting. "Not fair."

"Who said life is fair?" He scooted a little bit closer, cursing the armrest that stood in his way. She tensed, but didn't move away. "Tell me what your boyfriend would be doing right now, if he was here instead of me."

"Why bother? He's fake."

He shook his head and sighed. "But for the purpose of your family, he's real. How about we use the rest of the flight to come up with realistic stories? I'll be your muse."

She rolled her eyes. "Okay. If you were my boyfriend, you'd be doing exactly what you're doing. Touching me. Kissing me. Making me forget I'm about to crash to my fiery death. You know. Boyfriend crap."

After glancing around and making sure the stewardess wasn't behind him and that the rest of the passengers weren't watching, he cupped her cheeks and looked into her eyes. "If you remember the fact that you might die soon, then I'm not doing a good enough job, am I?"

A flush spread out from underneath his fingers to her nose and she scooted back a little bit. "I didn't mean—"

"Too late." His heart pounded in his ears, pronouncing his desire for her with each racing beat. Hoping he wasn't completely misreading her attraction to him, he leaned forward and melded her mouth to his again. She sighed and opened to him, and he threaded his hands into her hair. He kept the kiss light and teasing, pulling away to suck her lower lip.

Releasing her, he tried to take a deep breath. "Christ, you taste so damn good."

He didn't want her to think he was trying to get her into bed, nor did he want to take advantage of her when she was tipsy. But truthfully, he kind of *was* trying to get her into bed. Even if he hadn't been originally.

His intentions were no longer crystal clear.

"If I taste so good, then why did you stop?"

She grabbed him by the back of the neck and pulled him down again. As soon as their lips touched, her tongue was in his mouth. His gut clenched down hard, twisting and turning with need. She kissed him as if she couldn't get enough. Like she might even want him as much as he wanted her.

She shifted closer—or as close as she could get with the seat divider between them—and her nails raked down his sweater. She then slid her hands underneath the hem, touching bare skin. When she caressed his chest, he reached under the blanket and ran his fingers up her thigh and under her skirt. He brushed against her panties, just a little bit, and she whimpered in response.

Footsteps approached, and he froze.

Was he really doing this with her, on a plane where anyone could see them? What the hell was wrong with him? She deserved better than a public groping. She should have flowers and jewelry and a real hero instead of someone masquerading as one.

He let go of her and extracted his hand from between her legs. "Flight attendant," he whispered.

Kayla covered her face with shaking hands. With a little squeak, she cried into her hands, "Oh my God. I'm sorry."

"Don't apologize. You didn't do anything wrong. You don't have to feel bad."

"Yes, I did," she moaned through her hands. "I don't

even know you."

"You know enough. Trust me." He reached out to squeeze her thigh, and she scooted back from him as if his touch would burn her skin.

"Can I get you two anything else?" the attendant asked, eyeing Kayla's covered face with concern, then looking at the blanket that covered them both. "Everything okay?"

He tried to sound poised and calm, but need was ripping through him like a knife. "No thanks. We're good."

The flight attendant hesitated. "Can I get you anything, miss?"

"No, I'm fine," Kayla muttered. Though the attendant looked uncertain of this, she turned around and left. After they were alone again, Kayla dropped her hands and watched him as if he might bite. "I don't do this. This isn't me. I don't kiss strangers on planes."

He couldn't help but notice the last word was more of a whisper than a word. "Then we can wait till we're off," he said quickly.

She laughed and smacked his arm. "You know what I mean."

Reaching out, he grabbed her hands and squeezed them both. "It was just a kiss. We don't have to do it again if you don't want to."

"I don't." She flushed and bit down on her lower lip. "But, God help me, I do."

Oh, thank God. His ego had been taking a hit for a second. "You're over-thinking again."

"You're right. It was nothing."

Well, he wouldn't say that…

"Right." He raised a brow. "It's not like there's an actuary law against kissing ex-Marines. Or is there? Will you be fired or arrested? Burned in the town square as an example?"

"Don't be ridiculous. Of course there isn't," she huffed. Then her lips turned up. "But if there was, I'd *so* be on that stake."

He grinned. "I'm going to tell you something about *me* now. I don't often kiss girls on planes, either, but you're fucking beautiful and interesting as hell. I can't remember the last time I had so much fun with someone. If you want to kiss me again, then I'm here waiting. If not, that's fine, too."

She opened her mouth, started to speak, then gave a slight shake of her head. "I might want to, but I won't."

"I think you're protesting too much." But at least she *wanted* to kiss him, and this passion wasn't one sided. "You don't want a relationship, and neither do I. And I'm leaving the country next week. Some might say our situation is perfect for both of us."

She eyed him suspiciously and sank back against the seat. "I just don't think it's a good idea."

"How about if we go back to the topic of your fake boyfriend. We need to flesh him out more. You want him to be realistic, right?"

She dropped her head back on the seat and closed her eyes. "Yeah…I guess."

"Then how about we base your guy on me? You ask me any questions you want, and I'll answer them truthfully. Then, when you're with your family the answers will come easily."

She pursed her lips and shifted in the seat. She probably thought through everything she ever did in terms of risk assessment. He had a feeling she'd already done so with him, and kissing a guy she would never see again probably fell into the bad ideas section of her brain.

She needed to loosen up some.

Kayla opened her eyes and scrunched her nose. "Let me get this straight, you want me to build the character of my fake boyfriend around a guy I met at the airport and let grope me on my flight?"

"Yep." Watching her out of the corner of his eyes, he added, "If you didn't tell them a name yet, you can even use my name. You can use *me* in any way you desire."

Something flashed in her eyes. Something that he liked. "Any way?"

She called to him like a siren without even trying. Leaning so close that their noses practically touched, he held onto her gaze and traced a finger down her cheek.

"Any way. Anywhere. Anytime."

Chapter Four

Wow. He wasn't afraid to put it all out there.

Coming from a family with military men herself, she'd known a heck of a lot of service men over her years, and none of them had acted so carefree and seductive. They'd been harsh. Serious. Not like Cooper. He was so delightful that she wanted nothing more than to let him have his way with her.

He was so handsome. She couldn't resist thinking how explosive they could be together. Numerous times. Numerous ways. On the bed, kneeling in front of the couch, bent over the kitchen table, maybe even on the airplane…

No. She was *not* joining the mile-high club.

Giving herself a slight shake, she picked up her drink and gulped it down. "So you want me to use you, huh?"

He eyed her as he took a sip of his cocktail. As he moved the cup away from his mouth, he licked the moisture off his lips. She couldn't look away. He said, "Are you talking about asking me questions, or using me in a different way? Either way, the answer is *yes*."

She was tempted to do both. This had short-term written all over it, and that's how she liked her relationships. Short and sweet. "I think we'll start with questions for now."

He shrugged a shoulder. "Suit yourself."

She studied him. "How old are you?"

"Twenty-nine. I graduated college from University of Maine and then a few years later joined the Marines at my father's urging. You?"

"Twenty-seven." She pointed a finger at him. "But this is about you. Not me. Are your parents still married?"

"Yes, very happily so."

"Was your father in the military, too?"

"Yes, he was a career officer, and he hasn't stopped reminding me of that since I decided not to reenlist." Twisting his lips sardonically, he raised his glass to her. "The captain didn't approve of his only son deciding the military wasn't for him. After being under his thumb all my life, the military wasn't much of a challenge."

She nodded. "Why did you decide to get out of the Marines?"

He tensed. "I don't want to talk about that. Anything but that."

"Okay." She might be dying to know what brought the hardness to his voice, but she knew when to back off. "What does your father think of your new job?"

He scoffed. "He thinks I'm wasting my time. He owns a company for former military operatives. A private security detail. And he wanted me—"

"To run it." The puzzle that was Cooper rapidly came

together. He didn't seem like the type to accept things being handed to him. And he didn't strike her as kind of guy who would take the easy way out. She appreciated that in a man. "I'm guessing you're not interested?"

"Nope." He tossed back the remains of his drink and set the glass down. Clearly he didn't like the topic. "I'm not taking the position because I'm his son and a shoo-in. That's not fair to anyone. If I take a job, it's because I've proven myself to be the best candidate. No other reason."

So, she'd been right. Kayla took a sip of her drink and sat back. "What's your biggest fear?"

"Failure." He tightened his fists and looked down at his lap. "In particular, failure that will result in a loss of life."

She studied his lowered head, reached out and rested her hand on his knee. "Did you lose someone in the war that was close to you? A squad member, perhaps?"

He chuckled and tugged on a piece of her hair, making her stomach tighten. Such a simple gesture, but its effects were staggering. "You're persistent, I'll give you that. But this topic is closed, sweetheart."

"Fine." She withdrew her hand. "Then give me the biggest fear besides the one I'm not allowed to ask about?"

He leaned in closer. "It's a good fear. Humiliating, even. But it'll cost you."

"What's the price?"

"A kiss," he whispered.

Ha. She would've done that for nothing. "People will see."

"It's not like we haven't done that already. Besides, no one's watching us." He gestured at the other passengers. He was right. Most of them were sleeping or reading. No one was even remotely interested in the two of them. "Just one little kiss…"

Reaching out, she touched his hair. It was as soft as it looked, even though she'd first thought he had to use a whole can of hairspray to get it to fall so perfectly into place. No, he seemed to be naturally lucky with his hair. His face. His body. *Everything*, really.

She sighed, as if he was asking a lot of her. Let him stew on that. "Fine."

Grabbing on to his shoulders, she melded her lips against his, kissing him with all of the pent up frustration and need coursing through her veins.

For the next few days, she'd have to be the Kayla Moriarity that her whole family thought she was. The girl they all thought hadn't grown up yet. Tonight, on the plane with Cooper, would be all about *her*. The real her.

He trailed his fingers lightly over her shoulder. When his hands closed around her sides, his grip so close to her breasts, she arched her back in invitation. He seemed to get the hint. He lifted the blanket up over their shoulders and then closed his palms over her completely.

They broke apart when someone coughed. He slid his hands away from her, and the blanket fell back to their laps. Kayla scanned the passengers, looking for any signs that they knew the two people in the back row were *this close* to getting it on.

No one was watching. Unbelievable.

She took a shaky breath and met his eyes. The way they blazed back at her almost broke her resolve to not strip naked here and now. "I think I more than earned your secret, didn't I?"

"Hot damn." He dropped his head back against the plane seat. Dragging his hand down his face, he shot her a disgruntled look and adjusted his position on the seat. She totally wanted to peek under the blanket and see how hard he was right now. "My secret is I'm terrified of public speaking. When I get up in front of a crowd of people, or someone hands me a microphone, I panic. And I'm not talking about babbling like a fool or anything. I just stand there. Not moving. Not talking. Nothing."

She hadn't expected that. To think he was scared of anything seemed ludicrous, but of *speaking?* The man had a natural charm that drew her in—certainly it worked on other people. "Seriously?"

He nodded. "One time at a Marine Corps Ball, they decided I should give a speech for the commander. I have a feeling my buddies had something to do with that, though they denied it." He twisted his lips, his cheeks turning a little bit red. "One second, I'm sipping my drink and flirting with my date, the next they're announcing my name and calling me up to the stage. I didn't make a single intelligible peep, and I might have trembled under the spotlight, too. It was horrible. Needless to say, I went home alone that night."

"Oh, man." She covered her mouth with her hands to hide her grin. "That's just wrong. I would've still gone home with you."

He looked at her in surprise. "You would have?"

She nodded. "Totally. I like seeing weakness in men. It makes them more approachable."

He gently ran his fingers through her curls, and tingles shot through her body. He seemed to like touching her hair, and she liked him playing with it. "I also suck at dancing. I tend to avoid it with a cold, bad-boy demeanor, but the truth is I'm horrible at it. Sometimes, I wish I could dance."

"If there was room on this plane, I could help you with that. I happen to be an excellent dancer. My mom enrolled us in classes as kids."

"Too bad we won't see each other again. I'd take you up on that offer."

She frowned and looked out the window. "Maybe I could show you after the flight lands? A quickie in the parking lot?"

His lips curved upwards and he dropped her hair. "I think your definition of quickie differs from mine."

She met his eyes. "Are you so sure about that?"

"Kayla…" The smile faded away, and he cupped her cheek. "We could keep this easy or." His hand tightened on her. "We can make this a night to remember. Your choice."

Her heart sped up, and she looked away from him. "How long have you been single?"

"I refuse to be in a relationship when I deploy, and I've been deploying every year. So, suffice it to say I've been single for some time now. What about you?"

"I haven't had, or wanted, a boyfriend in a ridiculously long time."

"How long?

"Since college." She fidgeted with her skirt some more, not looking up at him. "I've had a few meaningless encounters—friends with benefits—but no real relationships. But it's by choice."

"Why is that?"

"I really don't believe in the institute of marriage being the thing that makes a woman whole. My old-fashioned family seems to think the only way I can be happy is if I have a man holding me up. Why should I encourage their limited views of the world by settling down with a guy who fits the part? You know, I saw so many childhood friends marry the first guy who came along just to have that 'special day.' But *every* day is *my* special day. I'm happy on my own." She looked out the window. There was another reason she wasn't being honest about. She might as well give him the whole answer since she'd told him everything else about herself minus her freaking bra size. "Plus, there's the whole issue of love."

He shifted his weight. "Meaning?"

"Well, I haven't fallen in love yet — not like everyone else I know has. Not even close." She straightened her shoulders and lifted her chin defiantly. "I'm beginning to wonder if I ever will, thus the reason I'm focusing more on myself at this point in my life. I don't think I'm a good fit with the emotion. It requires too much blind trust and warm gushy feelings, while I prefer logic and cold calculations."

"Yeah, that much is true. It's hard to let go like that." He snorted. "But you don't actually not believe in love, right? I mean, you know it's real."

"It's not that I don't believe in it, per se. It's just that I haven't been given a reason to think it'll happen to me, is all." She shrugged and tried to come up with a way to express exactly what she meant. "I've seen people fall in love, and I've seen people change for love. But *I* haven't done it. *I* haven't felt it. Maybe it's real, but it's just not real for *me*."

He shook his head. "I find it hard to believe a woman like you will never find love. You're kind, funny, and charming. Basically, you're the perfect catch." He reached out and covered her hand with his, squeezing gently. "If there's no hope for you, then how do the rest of us stand a chance in hell at a happy ending?"

"Who said I'm not happy now? It's not like I'm on a one-way ride to miserable Spinsterville." Her lips quirked at the corners.

He laughed. "Touché. Besides, I doubt a woman as amazing as you could ever find a man who deserved you. He doesn't exist."

"Oh really?"

"Really." His dimple flashed and Kayla melted. "You're incomparable."

While she wasn't unhappy with her life, she was certainly happier now that she'd met him. Without thinking, she wrapped her hands around the back of his neck and brought his mouth to hers, kissing him gently. That was such a sweet thing to say that she couldn't resist him anymore. Yeah, it pretty much sealed the deal in her eyes.

She was going home with him tonight.

Chapter Five

Cooper closed his hands around Kayla's waist. This was the second time she kissed him all on her own, and each time the desire inside of him grew closer to boiling over. He was pushing his restraint to the max, but he couldn't resist her. She might be warm and welcoming now, but once her feet were on solid ground again, she would return to her senses.

Once she wasn't afraid of dying.

But if he could make her come apart in his arms one time before they parted, he'd be happy. He slid his hand under the blanket again, his fingers trailing over the soft skin of her upper thigh.

She gasped when his palm made contact with her bare leg, but he kept his lips pressed against hers. Her legs parted under the blanket, and he slid his fingers higher, brushing against the soft satin of her panties. Something inside of him demanded he show her how good he could make her feel before she walked away from him forever.

Something to remember him by.

He didn't have much time to waste—it wasn't a particularly long flight from Maine to North Carolina—but if he was right, she would be ready. Slipping his fingers inside her panties, he felt her dampen his fingers instantly. He deepened his kiss and thrust his fingers deep inside her, thanking God for the dim lights, distracted passengers, and the blanket.

But still...he had to make it less obvious what he was doing.

He broke off and whispered in her ear, "Don't you move or make any noise. I'm going to make you come, but you can't make a sound. Got it?"

She nodded frantically, her breath coming out fast and soft.

He reached into the seat pocket with his free hand and opened up a SkyMall magazine on his lap, staring down at it as his fingers worked over her. "Close your eyes," Cooper whispered, his focus on the seat in front of him. "Pretend you're asleep."

She slammed her eyes shut and bit down on her lip, her pussy clenching down all around him as he rubbed his thumb against her clit. She was so tight and hot and wet...

He held back a groan when she squirmed, her body restlessly begging him for more. He moved his thumb over her clit even harder, making sure to keep pressure there, while thrusting inside of her with his fingers. Harder. Faster.

Fuck, she was going to kill him with those tiny little breaths she kept letting out.

She rocked her hips as he moved within her, and he lifted a knee under the blanket to hide her frantic movements. He could tell by the way her tight pussy was clenching down on his fingers that she was close. So fucking close. And damn if he wasn't close to ruining his damn pants, too, just from touching her.

He wished more than anything that they weren't on an airplane right now.

If only they were in a hotel room where she could scream his name without holding back. Where he could make her beg for his touch. Where he could do more.

"Come for me," he whispered, thrusting harder and pressing his thumb more insistently against her.

"C-Cooper," she whispered, her voice barely audible.

He glanced around, making sure no one heard, then returned his attention to her flushed face. She looked so damn erotic right now, on the precipice of orgasm. She bit down harder on her lip, and he wished more than ever that his cock could be buried inside her when she came.

"Yes. That's it," he whispered, scraping his thumb against her sensitive clit. She pumped her hips one last time, and then her body went tense, her pussy squeezing down on him as she exploded. He didn't let up on her once she relaxed, instead he brushed his thumb over her clit and wiggled his fingers again.

She tensed again, her cheeks even more red, and this time he withdrew his hand from between her legs. She collapsed against her seat, breathing heavily. Satisfaction poured through his veins.

The fasten seatbelts sign came on with a ding. Kayla's eyes went wide, and he saw a mixture of awe and embarrassment in her expression. "Oh my God."

He offered her an easy grin, even though his blood was

pounding in his head and his cock was so fucking hard it hurt to move. "Now buckle up. We're about to land, if I'm not mistaken."

She tugged down her skirt and fastened her seatbelt with shaking fingers, and he busied himself with adjusting his khakis to allow room for his painful erection. Jesus Christ, he'd never been so turned on in his life.

And yet…even he was a little shocked at what they'd just done. Hell, he didn't go around fucking women in public. Granted, he didn't actually fuck her, but *still*.

He'd made her come — on an airplane, of all places.

What had gotten into him? And why couldn't he wait to get his hands on her again? On the plane, in the airport, in a hotel. He didn't care where or when, but he needed more. She intoxicated him in every way.

He drew in a deep breath and looked at her, prepared for anything from tears to anger. Instead, she held up one of her crazy little wipes at him, her eyes on his hands, as calm as can be. "Here. For your hand."

He let out a short laugh then swallowed it down. He'd expected her to panic about landing or about, oh, he didn't know, fucking *coming* in front of a whole plane, and she handed him a sanitary wipe? The woman was unbelievable. "Seriously?"

She turned beet red. "Sure, why not?"

He took the wipe from her and cleaned his fingers, his thoughts scattered. "You have something for any situation in that thing, don't you?"

"Pretty much." She shrugged and dropped her gaze. Then peeked back up at him from behind her hair. "I like to be prepared. Oh, and thanks, by the way. For all the distracting." She flushed even more. "You went above and beyond the call of duty. So…yeah. Thanks."

"Don't mention it," he said dryly.

The way she clutched her hands together tightly told him all he needed to know about her. She might pretend that it wasn't a huge issue to her, but she was clearly nervous as hell. Their eyes met, but instead of calming him down… she fueled him on.

She might think this was the end of their time together, but if he had anything to say about it…it was only the beginning.

• • •

Well, that had certainly been a plane ride like no other.

Ever since Cooper had made her come with his fingers and a few whispered words, she'd been at a loss for what to say. He seemed to accept this without question, though. In fact, he'd been holding her hand and comforting her as they descended.

Who was this man, and what planet did he come from? In her experience, men like Cooper weren't real. They existed purely in the pages of romance novels and chick flicks.

But here he was. In the flesh. Driving her crazy with need.

What was she supposed to do with him now?

The plane jostled as it touched ground, and he fisted his hand in his lap. "Looks like we made it alive. No fiery crashes, and no watery grave."

"Thank God." She sat up straight and cleared her throat. "Thank you, again, for…well, everything." And for the mind-blowing orgasm. *Definitely* for the orgasm.

His lips quirked, almost as if he'd read her mind. "You're welcome."

The attendant's voice came over the speaker, welcoming them to North Carolina. Cooper looked at Kayla. She stared back. After a moment, she broke the silence. "What now?"

"Now we wait to get off." He looked over his shoulder and tapped his foot impatiently.

She snorted. "I thought I already did."

A chuckle escaped him. "Get your mind out of the gutter."

"All right, everyone," the flight attendant said from the front of the plane, her eyes skimming over all of the passengers. Kayla couldn't help but wonder if she *knew* what they had been up to in that back row. "Please watch your step on the jet bridge as you exit the plane."

Kayla stood up clumsily, cursing her legs for feeling so damned weak and shaky. "We made it in one piece."

"Indeed we did. After you." Cooper motioned her forward, waiting for her to clear the aisle. Then he grabbed his carry-on out of the overhead bin and followed her. "So, did you rent a car, or are your parents picking you up?"

Kayla looked over her shoulder at him. "No car for me. I'm catching the shuttle to a nearby hotel, where I'll be staying for the next few days. I'll call my mom to pick me up in the morning, when they're awake. She wanted to come tonight, but I decided to take a night to recover from the flight before I got swept up in the wedding madness."

He scratched the back of his head, looking utterly adorable with his tussled hair and sleepy eyes. Damn, but not many men could pull off that look. She was staring so hard as she walked, she tripped over a child's seat that was waiting to be picked up in the jet bridge.

"Watch it!" he called, just as she stumbled forward.

She righted herself quickly, trying to hide her embarrassment. "I'm okay."

He caught him fighting back a grin. "Good. That car seat came out of nowhere, huh?"

After that, they walked the rest of the way up the jet bridge in silence until they reached the gate. "Do you have baggage to pick up?" she asked.

"No, this is all I brought." he said, gesturing to his bag. "But I'll go with you to the baggage carousel if you want. If not, that's okay, too."

Oh, she wanted, all right. The question was, did he? He hadn't said a word about continuing what they'd started on the plane somewhere else yet. But he hadn't walked away yet, either.

So that meant something, right?

"Sure, come on." She took a step, then remembered something he'd said to her earlier. "Wait, you said you would see me after the flight. If you didn't have baggage to collect, then why did you say you'd see me again? Did you lie to me?"

"No." He shifted on his feet. "I would've come to check on you."

"Even though you didn't need any luggage?"

He met her eyes. "Yep. I would've made sure you were all right before I left. I don't make empty promises. If I say I'll see you later, I'll see you later."

"Oh." Her heart melted even more. He was oh-so-dangerous to her well-being with all his heroic thoughts and his magical orgasm-inducing fingers. She might as well climb out of her underwear and straddle him now, because that's how tonight was going to end if they didn't part ways soon. "I see."

He fell into step beside her. "After we're done here, I need to grab the keys for my rental. Want to come with me? I can drop you off at your hotel."

That sounded promising. "Okay."

She couldn't wait to bring him back to a hotel for one hell of a night.

Chapter Six

After picking up the key from the rental car desk, Cooper followed Kayla outside, wheeling her suitcase behind him. She'd been quiet ever since they landed. He wasn't sure what was going on in that pretty little head of hers, but he was dying to know.

He didn't want to walk away yet.

He swallowed hard and glanced up at the moon. It seemed just as unreachable as the beauty in front of him. "My car is in spot 123C."

She pointed off to a row across the lot. "There's row C."

"Yeah, I think I see my ride." When she headed in that direction, he picked up speed so he could walk beside her.

There was no other car near his rental, which made sense considering the hour. It had to be pushing one in the morning, if not later. In fact, the only reason the front desk was still open was because he'd asked if they'd wait for him to arrive. Now that he'd picked up the key, even the desk attendant had turned off the building lights and was nowhere to be found.

Halting mid-step, she grabbed his arm, stopping him in his tracks, too. "Wait. Should you be driving?"

He cocked his head. "Why wouldn't I be okay to drive?"

"You were drinking."

He snorted. "I didn't drink as much as you did. You didn't notice, but I stopped drinking a while ago. I'm sober as a clergyman."

"Oh."

"So, want that ride or not?"

When she nodded, anticipation shot through his body. Moments later, they reached his car. He loaded their bags and unlocked the doors so they could get in, and then tossed his jacket in the seat. Before he could climb in the driver's side, she came up to him and held out her arms. "You ready?"

He eyed her. "For?"

"Dancing, of course."

"*Haha*. Real funny." But then he realized she wasn't kidding at all. "Wait. You really want to do this? I might break your foot."

"Of course I want to! Consider it payment for helping me tonight." She flushed as soon as the words were out of her mouth. Even in this dim lighting he could see that. "For keeping me talking, I mean."

He walked up to her and placed his hands on her hips. "All right. Show me." He moved so close her chest brushed his. "I'm ready if you are."

Setting a hand on his shoulder, she instructed, "Hold my hand, but leave the other one on my hip."

He did as told, slipping his leg between hers. He had a

pretty good idea that he wasn't supposed to do that for a proper dance, but she didn't correct him. "Okay. What now?"

"Now, we take two steps forward, two steps back…" She followed him as he did what she told him, her body moving with a grace he'd never possess. "Good. Keep going, but move around as if we're on a ballroom floor, instead of staying in this spot."

He spun her in a dramatic circle, sweeping across the length of a parking spot. She giggled, her eyes shining up at him in the moonlight. He repeated the movement, making a wide arc around the car. Her hand fit perfectly in his, as if she were made to be his.

When he dipped her over his arm, she laughed and lifted her head, looking up at him. "Are you sure you haven't done this before?"

"Quite." Her happiness distracted him so much he stumbled over his own feet. They clung to each other, breathing heavily, their noses touching. He swallowed hard, his eyes latched on hers. "You know, I do know one type of dancing that you might not."

She licked her lips.

"What kind of dance is that?" she asked, her voice throaty and sexy as hell.

He pulled her upright without warning, until she rested on his upper thigh. "Follow my lead."

"Okay," she breathed.

Leaning down, he brushed his lips over hers then did a dip, supporting her lower back with his hand. To his surprise, she relaxed, lifting her breasts to his view without any effort. He eased her back up and kissed her neck, rotating his hips against hers.

She moaned and held on tight. As she moved against his leg, she dug her fingers into his shoulders. He dipped her again. This time, she fluidly bent so far backward he immediately dropped his head and nipped the sliver of skin exposed above the neckline of her sweater. Damn, she tasted so good, he had a hard time moving away from her.

He ran his free hand up her side, closing his palm around her breast. The damn turtleneck needed to go. He ached to put his mouth where his hand was. She gasped and lifted back up, her hands closing on the back of his neck.

Melding her lips to his, she slipped her tongue inside with a sigh. He groaned and stumbled back, slamming against the car. Her wool coat fell open and he slid his hands inside it. Swinging her around without breaking their kiss, he pressed her up against the SUV and lifted her legs. She wrapped their long length around him, opening herself to him, and he almost shouted with joy.

Nibbling on her ear, he said, "I want you. Now." He traced the curve of her breasts. Fucking A, the woman was perfection

"Yes," she sighed. She squeezed his arms. "Now."

Sweet Jesus, there was a God. Rolling his hips against hers again, he reached for the handle. It was time to finish what they'd started on that plane.

Chapter Seven

Kayla wrapped her legs around Cooper's waist, quivering from the desire he sparked in her. She'd never wanted someone so badly that she couldn't even wait ten short minutes to get to a hotel room. She knew it was freaking freezing outside, but she didn't feel a thing with how hot he was making her. Her whole body tingled with awareness. Awareness of *him*.

She had to have him. Right here. Right now.

Nothing else mattered.

He opened the car door and laid her gently on the backseat, pushing her sweater up and kissing her stomach. Bending down further, he licked the insides of her thighs and kissed his way up her leg. When he flicked his tongue over her already drenched panties, she cried out and dug her nails into his scalp. "Oh my God, Cooper. Yes."

He shoved the silken material aside, closing his mouth over her clit. She arched her hips, the pleasure consuming her within seconds. As his tongue worked over her, making her climb higher and higher, she tightened her thighs on his head to keep him in place. If he stopped now, she just might die.

His finger slipped inside her, and she threw her head back, a cry escaping her lips as she came explosively. She clawed at him, tugging him up. "Please. Fuck me."

He bit off a curse and crawled over her, slamming the door shut behind him.

Smashing his lips down on hers, he lowered himself between her legs, his hard cock pressing against her. When his tongue flicked hers at the same time as his cock pressed against her sensitive clit, she cried out and raised her hips. She could taste herself on his tongue, along with his masculine flavor, which she'd grown accustomed to over the past few hours.

It was an intoxicating mix.

Pure pleasure shot through her veins, rich and heady and addictive.

God, he knew the perfect way to touch her, to leave her trembling and on the brink of orgasm within seconds, even though she'd just been there what felt like only minutes before. Trailing her hands down his shoulders, over his pecs, and to his waist, she tugged the sweater up.

Tearing her mouth free, she panted, "Take it off. I want to see you."

"I will if you will," he said, stealing one last kiss before he pushed off of her. He perched on the edge of the seat between her legs and yanked his sweater off. The peek at his six-pack she'd gotten earlier was just a sneak preview of the full show. His muscle-ripped body surpassed her expectation. She reached up and traced the lines of his stomach with both hands, all the way down to the waist of his khakis. Hard. Hot. Pure man. He closed his eyes and his abs clenched. She watched him, mesmerized by the harsh planes of his body, and skimmed her fingers over his cock. With a tortured groan, he captured her hand and held it still against him. "You better stop that if you want me to take my time."

"I don't." She yanked free from his grip and cupped him again, massaging his cock through his pants. "I want you to fuck me."

"Kayla... Christ, that feels good."

Holy crap, he was much bigger than she expected. Sure, he was tall and muscular, and he had the type of body and confidence that made her think he would be well-endowed, but this was...*wow*.

Shaking off the thought, she closed her fingers around him through the fabric, running her hand down his cock as best as she could. He leaned against the door and groaned, his hips moving into her touch. She couldn't decide if she wanted to spend hours torturing him or if she had to have him now.

Urgency won out.

She unbuttoned his pants, carefully unzipped them, and slid her hand inside his boxers, circling his smooth cock with her fingers. With her free hand, she tugged him back down by the neck and captured his mouth. He pressed her back on the seat.

His breath coming out heavy, he tore his mouth off of hers and nibbled a path down her jaw, all the way to the base of her throat. Everywhere his lips touched burned. She was on fire, and he was fanning the flames. He reached down and tugged up the fabric around her waist, divesting her of her turtleneck.

The cool air helped her burning flesh somewhat—until he touched her again. But if she was going down in flames, then he was coming with her. Her fingers moved over his length again, then slid down to the base of his cock.

He grunted and pulled her hand out of his pants, his jaw tight. "Enough." He slid his hand around her back and undid her bra with a flick of his wrist, then pulled it off her shoulders. It fell on the floor somewhere. "Holy shit. You're beautiful."

She squirmed, nearly screaming for him to stop staring and start *doing*. She didn't know what made this so intense, but she'd never felt so much at once.

Passion. Impatience. Hunger.

Settling in between her legs, he caught her mouth again and lowered his weight on her. *Finally*. But it still wasn't enough.

Wriggling underneath him, she grabbed him by the waist and yanked him down. When his bare skin brushed against her already sensitive nipples, she hissed at the contact. His eyes darkened, and he slid his hands under her ass, pulling her against him.

When their mouths were a breath apart, she demanded, "*Now*."

He growled and smashed his lips to hers, drinking of her mouth. When he broke away, she heard the crinkling of a condom wrapper and almost shouted with joy. Then his lips were back on hers, and he rubbed his cock against her clit.

He positioned himself at her pussy, then thrust inside

her a tiny bit before pulling out. *Oh, for the love of God.* How much longer would he torture her? She cried out in protest. He couldn't keep teasing her like this, damn it.

She lifted her hips. "Come *on*."

"You're not ready yet." He pressed against her again, teasing her with his cock.

Grabbing his hips, she pulled on them as hard as she could. When he refused to budge, she slammed her fists down on the seat. "Please *now*."

"Now," he agreed, his voice deep with promise.

He grabbed her wrists and pinned them above her head, then entered her, filling her so completely she cried out at the pleasure. Then he pressed even further inside her, his eyes closed, his grip on her tight. "Fuck, you feel good."

"Oh my God," she sighed, meeting him when he thrust again. As he withdrew, then shifted forward again, the familiar pressure built up rapidly, and she spread her thighs as wide as she could in a car to take more of him in. He moved faster. Her stomach clenched, twisting with pleasure.

"More! I need more!" she gasped. "Please fuck me hard."

Capturing her mouth, he thrust inside of her all the way, finally letting himself go. And this time, he didn't stop to tease her, or kiss her gently, or almost enter her.

She tore her hands free and dug her fingers into his ass, pulling him even closer. He rotated his hips and deepened his thrusts, until she finally held all of him. Her head kept hitting the car door because of how hard he drove inside of her, but she didn't care. As long as he kept doing what he was doing, then he could bend her any which way he wanted.

He increased the tempo, his breath coming out in spurts.

She screamed and went limp in his arms, pleasure taking over every molecule in her body.

She'd thought he was amazing with his lips and his fingers?

That had been nothing compared to *this*.

He pumped into her again, then one more time, and his body tensed as he found his own pleasure, his head thrown back and his eyes squeezed shut. When he dropped down to cover her body, he buried his face in her neck and placed a light kiss there. "Holy shit, Kayla."

She nodded and swallowed hard, not trusting her voice yet. She was no stranger to orgasms, but that was a whole new classification of pleasure.

"Want me to drop you off at your hotel now?"

She nodded. "Yes, please." Then she hesitated. This might be the best or the worst idea ever, but she was going for it either way. "Would you like to, uh, stay the night?"

He looked down at her, his face lighting up with a wide grin. "And spend the night making love to you in a real bed?"

Dear God, he might kill me.

Anticipation and desire fluttered in her belly. For the love of God, they'd just *finished* having sex. She didn't know what the hell he did to her, but it was something indescribable. Amazing. Addictive.

She nodded. "Pretty much."

Grinning, he said, "Fuck yeah. Let's go."

Chapter Eight

The incessant ringing of her cell phone penetrated the heavy fog of sleep hanging over Kayla's head, but she still resisted the pull to alertness. Her pounding head and cotton ball mouth didn't promise a pleasant morning, and she wanted to avoid the harsh realities of her hangover for as long as she could. Squeezing her eyes shut, she snuggled deeper into the warmth curled around her back, holding her tightly…

Wait. Holding her?

Her eyes flew open, and she blinked at the strange hotel room. The sunlight was excruciatingly bright to her sensitive eyes, and her head felt as if she had beaten it against a wall repeatedly. She stretched, then froze, when she saw the hairy, muscular arm thrown over her stomach. Who did the arm belong to?

Oh God.

Cooper.

With harsh reality, all of the events leading up to last

night when he'd agreed to go to her hotel—after having sex with him in the back of his rented Escalade—came crashing back. Had she done all that?

Judging from the fine-ass naked man in bed next to her... she'd have to go with a *yes* to that question. And she didn't regret a second of it, either. He'd been incredible and kind and mind-blowing in the sack. What was there to regret?

Nothing.

But in the light of day, it was still a bit...shocking. And she needed to plan an exit strategy.

Chatting it up with the guy she screwed in the parking lot didn't seem appealing.

It was time to slink away and smile through days of wedding planning and fights, knowing she'd gotten hers before slipping into the role of the big sister.

When her iPhone rang again, Kayla stiffened and carefully lifted Cooper's arm from her waist. The tattoos on his chest flexed and rippled, drawing her eye. Wait. Tattoos? How had she missed them before? They were *hot*. Inch by inch, she slid off the mattress and tiptoed across the room. Maybe she could answer it, call a cab, and make her escape before he woke up and caught her.

As she rounded the bottom of the bed, her steps feather light and excruciatingly slow, Cooper rolled over in bed without opening his eyes and grabbed her phone...which was right next to his on the nightstand. "It's yours."

She froze. "Uh, yeah. Thanks." She reached out and snatched her phone from his fingers, making sure not to touch him. She didn't want to start something new with him this morning—something that led to talking and getting to know each other more intimately.

They'd already been plenty intimate.

"Hello?"

"Where are you? It's ten o'clock!" Her mother's voice boomed through the speaker and she momentarily pulled the phone away from her ear.

"Uh...at the hotel." She looked at Cooper's bare back. No tattoos there, but a hell of a lot of muscles that made her mouth water. *Hot damn*. He hadn't moved. Had he fallen back asleep? "I'm still in bed. My flight was late, and I slept in."

"That's very unlike you."

Kayla sighed. It wasn't. But it was unlike the "perfect daughter" she tried to be in front of them. She was so independent when she wasn't dealing with her family, but something about interacting with them tore her up. As pathetic as it sounded, it was just easier not to put up too much of a fuss with them. Then they all could happily part ways and she could return to her life in Maine until the next family visit. "I know. I'm sorry. I'll wash up and then I'll call you when I'm ready to be picked—"

"I can give you a ride." Cooper lifted his head and blinked at her. "They don't need to come out. I don't mind—"

Kayla held a finger over her mouth and gave him a hard look, so he cut off mid-sentence. She pointed to the phone, then held her breath and prayed her mom hadn't heard him. He'd spoken quietly. Really, *really* quietly.

But Kayla's mom had superhero hearing, and this time proved to be no exception. "Was that a man I just heard?"

"What? A man?" Kayla paced and forced a laugh. "No, of course it wasn't a man. It was the TV. That's all you heard."

"It didn't sound like the TV." Kayla heard a car door shut through the earpiece. "I'm coming over now."

"No, don't come yet. I'm not ready." Kayla stopped in front of Cooper and nudged him, glowering at him. "I'm alone."

Cooper sat up and rubbed his eyes. He looked confused as to why Kayla might be shooting daggers at him with her scowl. She gave him an even dirtier look.

"I don't believe you."

Kayla sighed. "Mom, if someone was here, why would I lie about it?"

"Well…" Her mom hesitated. "Did you and your boyfriend break up? What's his name, anyway?"

"Cooper. His name is Cooper," she said. Cooper's head snapped up, and he looked at her. "And no, we didn't break up. I'm alone, and you heard the TV."

"All right," her mom said.

"So I'll call you when I'm ready. Okay?"

Her mom fell silent. It seemed like she finally believed her. And then…

Another phone rang. Cooper's phone. And it was *loud*. Cooper scrambled to silence it, but it was too late. Her mother heard it. "I knew it. You're not alone."

Kayla sank onto the bed, looking at Cooper with panic coursing through her veins. "Mom…"

"Did you bring him? Is Cooper with you?"

He must have heard the question, because he grabbed Kayla's arm and nodded rapidly. Then he mouthed, "*Say yes. Tell her I'm here.*"

"Um…" Kayla blinked at him and shook her head. He nodded more enthusiastically. "Well…"

She took a deep breath. Did she dare? Was he suggesting she say her boyfriend was here? With her? But then what? Was he ready and willing to play the part? That seemed insane. He sighed and reached for the phone, but Kayla slapped his hand away. "You're right! It's Cooper! We wanted to…to…" Kayla looked at him.

He whispered, "Surprise you. Say it."

"We wanted to surprise you all," Kayla finished, watching him the whole time. "So don't come get me. We'll come together."

Cooper nodded.

"Oh, this is the best surprise ever." Her mom clapped and let out a *whoop*. "We're finally meeting him. I can't believe it! I'm going to tell *everyone*."

Kayla winced. "You don't have to—" The line clicked off. Her mom had hung up on her. "—tell everyone," Kayla finished to the dead line, lowering her phone to her lap.

Cooper grinned at her. He looked way too cheerful considering the circumstances. "So, I'm coming to the wedding?"

"Are you insane?" Kayla lurched to her feet. "Why in God's name would you offer to go to my sister's wedding with me?"

He shrugged, then his gaze dipped over her body. "I was the one who ruined your cover story. It felt right. You needed help, so I offered it."

"It felt *right*?" She threw her arms out to the side. "The knight in shining armor act was cute last night, and it was well-rewarded, I'd say." She gestured to the rumpled bed. "But now, even with the booze out of your system…how can you be this…this…sweet? Seriously?"

He cocked a brow. "I'm not fucking *sweet*. Puppies are fucking sweet. Not me."

It wasn't until Cooper cleared his throat and forced his eyes northward that Kayla remembered one tiny little detail. She was freaking *naked*. He might have seen it all last night when she'd had the courage of vodka in her, and she might have been A-Okay with that then.

But now, in the light of day?

Yeah, not so cool with it.

She whipped the comforter off of the bed and wrapped it around her shoulders. "Fine. You're not sweet. But what the hell are you?"

He shrugged. "I'm in town earlier than I need to be, so I have nothing to do besides wait to ship out. You needed a man, and since your family heard me over the phone, I offered to fill that position. We already get along nicely, and I've obviously enjoyed spending time with you," he said dryly. "So it's hardly a hardship for me to spend more time with you. That's who I am. That's *me*."

Kayla watched him. This guy, this man, was an anomaly. She couldn't read him at all. Ninety percent of single men would say anything—hell, do anything—to get laid. And the married men weren't much better. But *that* wasn't what he wanted. He'd already gotten that without asking. But he seemed to *care*.

What was she supposed to do with that?

He got out of bed, obviously not worried about his state of undress, and strode across the room wearing nothing but his tattoos. Grabbing a glass off the counter, he filled it with water. She knew she should look away from his bare ass, which was *not* inked, but she didn't want to. She wasn't *that* hung over. And, hell, if he was going to walk around with it all hanging out…who was she to complain?

"Let me guess," he said, his eyes on her as he crossed the room to his luggage. "You're no longer drunk, and now you're ready to bolt from the mistakes you made last night. In my car. In the bed that you're now refusing to look at. And, if I recall correctly, on that wall right next to you."

"Oh, God." She closed her eyes, each detail he named coming back with crystal clarity. "It's just…I don't *know* you."

He laughed. "You knew me well enough for me to make you scream my name repeatedly. Isn't that enough?"

"For a one night stand? It's plenty." She clutched the comforter tighter to her chest. "But for you to meet my family? My very traditional family who will badger you with questions every opportunity they get? Yeah, not so much."

"I fought in a war against enemies with deadly weapons. I think I can handle inquisitive parents."

"You've never met mine." She shook her head and headed for her luggage. "I really don't think you know what you're getting yourself into here. Thanks for offering to help me, but no thanks. I'd rather come up with some lame excuse now than have our story poked apart mid-ruse."

"I want to help you. Let me help you." He stepped in her path. "What are you going to tell them? I flew all the way down here, only to run away in the morning? That's not realistic."

"I've got it!" she said, thinking fast. "I'll tell them you got a call from work at the last minute—"

"No. Absolutely not." He crossed his arms. And he was still blessedly *naked*. Holy mother of God, those abs…she could freaking wash laundry on them. "At the very least, I have to show up for day one. Then I could get called away. If you try to play that off too soon, your mom will call you on it."

"What makes you so sure you know my mom so well?" He was right, but that wasn't the point. "You've never even met her."

"You told me all I needed to know last night. And I heard her on the phone." He grabbed her hands and squeezed. "Your mom is just like mine. I know how moms like that act. You don't want her getting suspicious. You'd spend the whole wedding dealing with the millions of questions she would throw your way. Let *me* take those questions. And you never know. Maybe if she sees you happy with someone, she'll focus on your sister, the bride."

Kayla bit down on her lip and studied him. "Do you seriously want to do this?"

"I do." He smiled at her, his eyes warm. "You want to know what's in it for me, but you're too polite to ask. Am I right?"

She laughed. "Now you can read me and my mom? If this wasn't a fake relationship, I'd *marry* you."

"You're moving way too fast for this fictional relationship." He chuckled and hugged her close. She almost pushed him away. It was too…too…real. Hugging was intimate. Hugging was for *actual* boyfriends and girlfriends.

She was much more comfortable keeping things purely sexual.

"I do want to know what's in it for you. I mean, you'll get free room and board, and good food." She looked down at her bare toes and wiggled them. "And more sex. But is that really worth dealing with my parents?"

He flinched. "Ouch. That almost hurts my ego that you have to ask me that question."

"As if your ego is that fragile. Puh-lease." She rolled her eyes. "Men that look like you and fuck like you aren't easily broken. You're as hard as your abs."

"Whoa, there. Hold up a second." He pressed a hand to his forehead, feigning shock. "That was *almost* a compliment. If you're not careful, I might think you actually like me."

Despite herself, she laughed. "You know, keeping you around might not be so bad after all. You're as entertaining out of bed as you are in it."

He raised a brow. "Then it's settled? I'm temporarily yours for the next few days?"

There was obviously no risk of her falling for him—he was leaving the country and she knew that already, so why would she put herself through a long distance relationship?

But what if the impossible became possible? What if one of them fell for the other?

She looked up at him, losing herself in his bright green eyes.

It just seemed a recipe for disaster.

Clearing her throat, she said, "Just to be clear. You, me… this is strictly platonic…with benefits."

"Exactly. No attachments," he agreed, lowering his face. His lips almost touched hers. "Just two people enjoying each other's company for a short time while pretending to be in love. What could possibly go wrong?"

She took a deep breath and gathered her courage, remembering his words from last night when she invited him to her hotel room. "Fuck yeah. Let's go."

Without warning, he took the step that closed the distance between them and his lips closed over hers, his tongue inside her mouth within seconds. All confident and hot.

Groaning, he swept her up in his arms, his lips still on hers. As he worked her mouth, he crossed the room and headed into the bathroom. When he set her down, her bare feet on the cold tile, she blinked up at him. Why did he put her down?

And worse yet—why wasn't he kissing her anymore?

Reaching past her, he turned on the shower, and the steam crept out from behind the shower curtain instantly. "Like I said, I'd like to stay with you. I want to spend the next couple of days giving you mind-blowing orgasms every night, if you'll let me."

"With an offer like that, you make it impossible to refuse."

And God help her, she didn't want to. Not when his naked body was against hers as the steam from the shower curled around them.

He appealed to her in an irresistible way. And, really, why was she resisting at all? It's not like she wanted a long-term relationship in her life, and this situation was perfect.

Simple. Easy. Painless.

Why not take what he had to offer?

Chapter Nine

When Kayla stood up on tiptoes and kissed him, her tongue brushing against his parted lips, Cooper knew their relationship ruse was a done deal. For better or for worse, they were doing this. He closed his arms around her, shoving down the blanket she'd wrapped around her shoulders earlier, until she stood in front of him as naked as he was.

Then he lifted her up over the tub and into the shower, not breaking contact with her mouth the whole way, even as he climbed in with her. When she hit the wall, he slid his hands under her ass and lifted her up. She wrapped her legs around his waist and surged against him, rubbing his cock between her legs. Desire pooled in his gut, fueled with a bout of desperation.

She dug her nails into his shoulders, pulling him tighter against her chest. The water cascaded over them, rolling down her neck and over her pink nipples. Fuck, that was a sight for sore eyes, right there.

One he never wanted to forget.

"Put me down," she demanded.

She wiggled in his arms, and he did as she requested. When he dropped her legs from his waist, she put her hands on his chest and backed him into the shower stream. He let her, because why the hell not? Whatever she had planned was sure to be beneficial to them both. She stood up on tiptoe, brushing her hard nipples against him teasingly, and she kissed him again.

He hissed in a deep breath as she slid her hand between their bodies and brushed her fingers against his cock. "You're going to kill me," he muttered, his jaw tight.

She grinned. "Perhaps. But I promise that you'll enjoy every second of it."

"I never doubted it."

The water ran down her forehead and made her long lashes spiky, drawing attention to her heated gaze. He gripped her waist, pulling her closer so he could touch her, but she slapped his hold off. "I'm in charge."

"We'll see about that," he said, his hold on her tight and his cock hurting from how hard he was. "But I'll allow it… for now."

She trailed her fingers down the thin line of hair that led to his cock. "Something tells me you like to be in charge at all times. Am I right?"

He flexed his jaw. "You're right."

"Hm. We'll have to fix that." She closed her hand over his shaft. "Sometimes it's nice to let go."

She released her hold on him and maneuvered him out of the shower stream. Then she picked up a washcloth and squirted some soap on it. He stood completely still and let her do what she wanted. She ran the washcloth over his chest then scrubbed his hard nipples. He hissed again and clenched his fists tighter, need building in his gut.

Yep. She was going to fucking kill him.

When she spun him around to face the wall, he glanced at her in confusion. He'd rather be watching *her*, damn it. "Kayla."

"Shh." Behind him, she trailed her fingers over his hard stomach, letting her wrist brush his cock, but nothing more. "Hands up on the wall."

Incredulous, he shot her a look over his shoulder. "Are you fucking kidding me?"

She pursed her lips and didn't say anything. As a matter of fact, she stared him the fuck down. Finally, after an internal struggle with himself, he turned back around and placed his hands on the wall. Leaning in, she washed his back, then moved the soapy washcloth over his ass. She cupped the muscles there as she rubbed her wet breasts against him.

That was *enough*.

He turned around, sweeping her into his arms and regaining control. She'd had her fun—now it was his turn to play. His mouth swooped down on hers, refusing to be told no. He cupped her ass and started to lift her against the wall, but she pulled free and shook her head.

"I'm not done yet," she breathed.

"Kayla…" He dropped his forehead to hers. "If you don't stop this torment soon, payback will be a bitch."

"Then I guess I better earn it, huh?" Sinking to her knees, she looked up at him through her lashes. "Don't move if you want to be inside of my mouth."

He stared down at her, his cock begging for what she was

about to do. He didn't move a muscle. "Fuck yeah, I want it."

With the washcloth, she rubbed his balls, taking her sweet time. By the time she was finished, he was panting erratically and his eyes were shut, and he was ready to beg.

Him. Begging. He didn't fucking beg, for Christ's sakes.

Dropping the washcloth, she pulled him forward into the water again. Once all traces of soap were gone, she ran her fingers over his cock. Then she flicked her tongue against the head, cupping his balls with her hands, and sucked him in so deeply he almost died.

He froze, his hands entwined in her wet locks. "*Kayla.*"

"I know." She ran her tongue up his cock, from the bottom to the tip, and he groaned. The noise sounded way too tortured for his liking. She was trying to break him…and succeeding. "But it hurts so good, doesn't it, Cooper?"

Her pink tongue darted out against his cock, driving him insane. Her eyes met his, and then she licked him again, this time running her tongue up his whole length. His voice raspy and rough, he said, "Do that again."

She did, and then she flicked her tongue over him, this time closing her fingers around him and squeezing. Swirling her tongue over the head of his cock, she took him deep into her mouth, sucking gently, and he almost came right then and there.

His thighs trembled and he collapsed against the shower wall, inviting the cold tile against his back. Maybe it would help him keep his head. But then she moaned and took him in even deeper. Without giving her a warning, he picked her up and set her on her feet, leaving about a foot between them.

When she took a step toward him, her eyes on his cock,

he held a hand out. "No. I'm *not* coming in your mouth, damn it. When I come, I'll be buried so deep in your pussy that you'll forget what it feels like to *not* have me inside of you."

She bit down on that lusciously swollen bottom lip of hers. "God, yes."

"And you'll be screaming that, too." He spun her around, his hands roaming over her full breasts, and then he pressed her forward against the cool tile wall. Just like she'd done to him. "Now it's *my* turn to play, sweetheart."

He slapped her ass lightly, then nibbled on her neck. She cried out and squeezed her legs together. "Oh my God."

He slapped her ass again, then spun her around to face him. Next, he framed her face with his hands and kissed her, devouring her mouth hungrily. She gripped his forearms as she returned his kiss.

Her tongue danced with his and a soft cry escaped her. He grabbed the washcloth she'd used earlier and slid it over her shoulder, slow and gentle. He squeezed her nipples through the fabric, tugging on them until she whimpered. Then he ripped his lips from hers and washed her stomach, his fingers dipping close to her clit, but not touching her. She needed to wait for that a little while longer after those tricks she'd played earlier.

Payback was a bitch.

He nibbled on her neck and ran the washcloth over her wet curls, then traced the curve of her ass. Man, he loved that ass of hers.

"*Now*," she demanded, lifting her leg so he could wash it. "Please."

He washed her inner thigh, slowly inching up to her

pussy. Dropping her leg, he lifted her other one. "Not yet."

Lowering his head, he closed his mouth around her nipple and scraped his teeth against it. She cradled the back of his head, pulling him closer. He dropped to his knees and nibbled at her hip, dipping the washcloth between her legs. Loving the way she looked from down here, all soapy wet and glistening.

He saw her knees tremble and she spread her legs more. Every touch, every caress, sent her closer to the edge—he knew it.

He rubbed his thumb against her clit, massaging her in slow circles, and her knees gave out. He saved her from hitting the floor with his free arm, supporting her weight since she couldn't at the moment. When she regained her footing, he stood and rinsed her off, then slammed his fist down on the shower knob, shutting off the water.

He picked her up and deposited her in front of the sink — and the mirror. Reaching past her, he grabbed a condom off the counter and rolled it on, his gaze locked with hers. "I'm going to fuck you, and I want you to watch the whole time."

She bit down hard on her lip and whimpered. She tried to hide it, but he heard it.

"But first…" He dropped to his knees in front of her and licked her, closing his eyes as he did. Her pussy tasted so fucking sweet. He gripped her hips and swirled his tongue against her clit, pressing deeper. Harder. She let out a cry, her hands digging into his scalp.

He lifted her hips a little more and increased the pressure with each swirl of his tongue, and then she went still, one word bursting out of her lips like a prayer. "Cooper."

She wasn't allowed to crash. She needed to keep soaring.

He stood, spun her so she was bent forward sprawled across the sink, and then slammed inside of her. Their gazes locked in the mirror, her flushed cheeks and swollen lips nearly sending him over the edge. He cupped her breasts, his thumb tweaking her nipples, as he moved inside of her with a desperation he'd never felt before.

Fuck, she was hot.

He withdrew and thrust forward again, groaning when her pussy clenched down on him. She was coming, and he was right there with her. He reached around her and pressed his thumb against her clit, applying a light pressure, and drove home inside her.

"*Oh my God*," she cried out.

His whole body gave way, and his cock jerked as he came. He buried his face in her neck, his arms tight around her. The pleasure shattered him into a million fucking pieces, and he collapsed against her back, making sure to put his weight on the sink instead of on her.

"Fuck."

He held her tight, closing his eyes and resting his cheek against her back. He couldn't help but realize that for the first time ever…

He didn't want to let a woman go.

Chapter Ten

Later that afternoon, Kayla looked out the window of Cooper's Escalade, tapping her fingers on the door. "When you meet my mom, make sure you're charming. Like, full blast. If you do that, there's an eighty-nine-point-nine percent chance that you'll distract her from asking you too many questions. And she might just fall for this whole thing, too. Maybe."

He laughed. "Is that so? That's an *awfully* precise number."

She shrugged. "I'm that good. And when you meet her, give her the dimples. They worked on me. Also, there's a seventy-three percent chance that—"

"Sweetheart? You're babbling again."

Her cheeks heated. He was right. She was. "I'm sorry. I just want this to go as smoothly as possible." She turned to him. "There's a seventy-three percent chance that my dad will hate you."

"You had to get that statistic out, didn't you?"

"Oh my God, yes."

He grinned and turned down the road that led to the restaurant where the rehearsal dinner was being held. "I think I can handle those odds. I'll manage to win over your mom, which will win over your dad. So don't worry."

"I didn't doubt you could do that," she said dryly. "Your charm is legendary already."

And they would need that charm in the face of her family's pending wrath. They hadn't made it to her parents' house before the dinner party. As a matter of fact, they'd been running behind ever since he'd seduced her into another round of sex this morning.

And *man*, what a round it had been.

She hoped there would be a lot more of that after they got through this party and returned to the hotel.

It would be her reward for good behavior.

"Well…" He bent down to peer through the windshield toward the restaurant. "Let's go over some more details real quick. When's your birthday?"

"May third." She looked back at him. "Yours?"

"December sixth." He turned into the parking lot. "Are we into PDA?"

She hesitated. "Hand holding and soft kisses. No tongue."

"Damn. I guess I'll have to behave myself until later, then."

"When we're alone, all bets are off." She skimmed her fingers over his thigh, creeping toward his cock but not touching him there. "But you already knew that."

"I did," he said, his voice a little raspy. "Are you allergic to anything?"

"Peanuts."

"Me too." He shot her a surprised look. "Looks like our fictional kids are fucked."

She laughed. "Guess so. But you're moving way too fast for this fictional relationship."

"Touché. Favorite food?"

"Steak and potatoes." She sighed as they pulled into the parking spot. She really didn't want to go inside. Didn't want to start this whole charade.

They were *so* going to fail.

In fact, she'd bet they had a ninety-four-point-six percent chance of failing—and that was being generous.

Why couldn't she be allowed to just enjoy her sister's wedding in peace? Without a date, people would bombard her with questions about when she was going to settle down. Yet with a date, she ran the risk of having people bombard her with the very same questions.

She was damned if she did. And damned if she didn't.

She checked her hair one more time. Lowering the visor, she asked, "Your favorite food?"

"Lobster and scallops." He unclicked his seatbelt. "Are we going with my real profession, or are we making up a more prestigious one?"

Surprised, she looked at him, her hand half-way to her face. "Private security and past Marine? It doesn't get any better than that in my family. They're big on military and service men."

"All right. So we're telling the truth? That I couldn't cut it in the Marines?"

She reached out and squeezed his thigh, but he still didn't look at her. "There's no shame in leaving the Corps.

Most of your co-workers at your new job will be the same as you. Private security primarily is made up of former military. And private security is okay with my family too. I'm sure of it." She hesitated, debating her next question about his time stationed abroad. "What happened over there anyway?"

He pressed his lips together. "Nothing. You ready to go in?"

No, she wasn't. She'd rather sit here and talk about his life some more, and about what had happened when he'd been overseas, but she knew he was done. The topic was closed, and she had to respect that.

She had a sinking suspicion he was running from something, or someone, as if he felt he owed a debt and he had to sacrifice his own happiness to pay it. But she wasn't going to push it. Now was not the time. Not after he was trying so hard to make tonight with her family easy for her.

"Let's do this." She opened the door and stepped out, her foot slipping on a patch of ice upon contact. Laughter and music trickled through the cracked door of the restaurant. Her parents had rented a hall out for the pre-wedding party. A few distant cousins huddled outside of the door, smoking and chatting. Normally, Kayla would be the responsible one. The one who took care of them all if they drank too much, making sure they all got into bed okay and didn't puke all over themselves.

But not this time.

This time, she was going to forget about them and enjoy her sister's wedding with Cooper at her side. She'd dance. She'd laugh. Maybe she'd even get a little drunk herself. Then, when she was done here, she would go home with Cooper and have crazy-ass orgasms all night long.

Take that, world.

Cooper came up to her side and slid his hand into hers. "What are the odds we'll fail?"

She hesitated. Maybe she should sugarcoat it for the sake of optimism and all that universe crap. "Fifty-fifty."

"Liar," he said under his breath. "Give it to me straight."

"Ninety-four-point-six, I'd say." She stole a peek at him. "How'd you know I was lying?"

"You blushed." He rubbed his jaw, his gaze on the restaurant door. "Do we love each other? How long have we been together?"

Kayla couldn't stop focusing on that word. *Love.* Coming from him, it sounded...hell, she didn't know. But it hit her hard for some reason. "Uh, yeah. We love each other. We should say it a few times, I guess. Get used to it. Lay it on me, big man."

He stopped walking, cupped her face, and met her eyes. "I...I...I can't. I've never said it to a woman other than my mother before, and when I do, I want it to be real. If I ever say I love someone, I'll mean it. I can't pretend that. But I'll make sure they can *see* we're in love."

The way he was looking at her felt an awful lot like love, so that could totally work. And knowing he'd never told anyone that he loved them before kind of made her happy.

What the hell was up with that? It wasn't as if he was ever going to say it to her.

They wouldn't know each other long enough to progress that far.

And for the first time, his upcoming move overseas didn't make her happy. It made her feel...*restless*. Itchy. She cleared her throat and forced a smile, covering his hand with hers. "As long as you can say it with your eyes, it works for me."

He wrinkled his brow. "Like this?" He gave her a smoldering look that would rival Ian Somerhalder. *Hot damn*. "How's that?"

Freaking breathtaking. But that wasn't *love* that his eyes were screaming at her. No, they were saying, *fuck me now*. And she wanted to oh so badly.

"Keep staring at me like that and I'll be sneaking you into the bathroom for a quickie." She quickly lowered her eyes. "But that kind of look's not what I meant. I was talking about the way you were watching me before. All warm, tender and sweet. As if you really cared about me."

"Sweet and tender?" He blinked in confusion. "I didn't realize I was looking at you that way. Maybe it was a trick of the lighting."

Her pulse kicked up a notch. "Oh."

"Yeah." He shook his head slightly and dropped his hand, seeming to be as confused as she felt right now. He stepped back from her and dragged a hand through his hair. "I'll try to recreate it, though."

"All right. Here we go."

He weaved his fingers through hers and led her inside. As soon as their feet crossed the threshold of the restaurant, her mother pounced on them with open arms. She must have been watching for their arrival. Buried in layers of red curly hair, and the familiar scent of Chanel perfume, her mother hugged Kayla tightly. She returned the embrace with the hand that wasn't still entwined with Cooper's.

For some reason, she didn't want to let go of him yet. "Hi, Mom."

"Sweetheart, we missed you at Christmas." Pulling back, she gazed at Cooper over Kayla's head, her mouth curved in a smile. "But now that I've met your infamous boyfriend, I can totally see why you stayed home. I would have, too."

Kayla's cheeks heated. Leave it to her mother to speak her mind without any censure. Very un-Southern of her. "Mom, this is Cooper Shillings. Cooper, my mother, Holly. I'm sure my dad will be along soon, too."

"Mrs. Moriarity, I'm happy to finally get to meet you." Cooper shook her hand. "I've heard so many wonderful things about you."

Her mom beamed up at him, holding his hand with both of hers. "And I've heard almost nothing about you." She quickly cut her eyes at Kayla, but her warm expression was firmly in place when she returned her gaze to Cooper. "I'm so pleased to meet you and so happy you could clear time in your schedule to join Kayla. Will you be staying for the whole weekend and the wedding?"

After her mother released his hand, he replied, "I do believe so, yes. I report for my new job on Monday, but I'll be here until then. Refresh my memory, what day is the wedding?"

"Saturday," Kayla offered quickly. Then she smiled at her mom, her heart racing. Already they were running into issues. He *should* have known when the wedding was, if he was really her boyfriend. "I hadn't told him since he wasn't coming originally. Besides, you know how men are with weddings."

"Right," Cooper agreed, taking Kayla's hand, his fingers flexing. "So, yes, I'll be here for the wedding, as long as the last minute addition doesn't cause any problems for you.

I know you've been busy making everything perfect for this weekend. Kayla told me how hard you work to make everyone happy, and you always succeed."

"Aw, well aren't you sweet?" Her mom melted. Literally melted into a puddle. "Of course I don't mind adding another person, dear. I'm thrilled to have you here."

"Excellent," he said, smiling.

"Come, let's introduce you to everyone else." Her mother met Cooper's eyes and offered a sympathetic expression. "But first Kayla's father is waiting to meet you, too. I apologize in advance."

Cooper shot Kayla an unreadable look as Kayla's mom headed across the room, towing a nervous looking Cooper behind her. "Should I be scared?" he whispered.

Kayla grimaced and nodded.

Her sister, Susan, rushed up to the group. Her brown hair was pulled back in an impeccable bun, and her blue eyes were latched on Cooper with surprise. "It's true? You brought your boyfriend with you! I thought you made him up to get Mom off your back."

"I'm right here," her mom said, not even bothering to act offended.

"I know, but even you have to admit it was dodgy that she wouldn't even tell us her boyfriend's name." She turned to Cooper. "Said she wanted everything about him to be a surprise for when we met him. Go figure."

"Well, I uh," Kayla fumbled, "I did."

"I see that *now*. But I also know how Mom is about digging into our personal life."

"Again, Susan. I'm right here," her mom interjected. "Besides, there's nothing wrong with my desire to see my children happily married. It's only natural. But now that we have Cooper—"

"*Mom!*" Kayla closed her eyes in mortification. Thank God this relationship wasn't real, or this conversation would be even more awkward than it already was. "Stop it."

"What? Marriage is something that every new couple should discuss up front." Her mom smiled at Cooper. "It's good to know where you stand early on, wouldn't you agree?"

"Absolutely, Mrs. Moriarity." He threw his hand over her shoulders. "Marriage is a very serious topic that one should never take lightly, and it's something we've discussed several times. We both know where we stand."

She smiled even bigger. "I'm glad to hear that."

"Stop torturing them, Mom." Susan hugged Kayla tightly, and Kayla held her close. When the hug ended, Susan motioned her fiancé, Max, over. "Cooper, it's great to meet you."

Cooper stepped forward, both dimples in full force just like Kayla had asked for. "It's lovely to meet you, too, Susan. Kayla and I are so happy for you and Max."

Kayla nodded. "*So* happy. I can't wait to see your dress, too. I mean, the picture you emailed was nice but I'm sure it's even more beautiful in person."

"I'll show it to you tomorrow when you come to dinner," Susan promised, grinning at them both. "Oh, here's Max."

"Kayla, you're here!" Max hugged Kayla, then turned to Cooper. His blond hair was longer than she remembered, and he was clean-shaven. He was a little shorter than Cooper, but not much, and he wore a black suit. He looked happily in love. "Hello, I'm Max."

"Cooper Shillings." Cooper shook his hand, inclining his head. "I'm the boyfriend who everyone thought was fake, apparently."

Max laughed. "Well, welcome to the family. Glad to see you're real."

"Thank you for having me."

Her mother clapped her hands and sighed, looking way too happy to have both the sisters and their men here together. "Susan and Max, you two have to mingle, since it's your wedding party. Off you go now."

Kayla kept Susan close. "But we just saw each other."

"You'll see each other again," her mom said primly.

Susan smiled at Kayla and smoothed her satin dress. The red was quite a lovely color on her. "We'll have more time tomorrow. There's a reason we took the day off before the wedding to relax." She counted off on her fingers. "Rehearsal dinner tonight, small family gathering at home tomorrow. A bit unorthodox, given that most rehearsal dinners are the night before. But it's my day and this is the way I wanted it."

Good for you for going after what you want, Kayla thought.

"Right. Now off you go, Susan." Her mom gently turned her in the opposite direction. "Cooper hasn't met your father yet."

"Oh." Susan looked over her shoulder at Cooper and cringed. "Good luck with that."

Cooper blinked at her. And he might have paled, too. "Uh, thanks?"

"He's not *that* bad," Kayla said to Susan. Then she looked at Cooper and tried her best to be reassuring. "He's really not."

"Yes, he is," her mom said sympathetically. "That's him, in the corner. Ignore any rudeness you might get—it's all in the name of his love for Kayla."

Kayla watched Cooper's eyes follow her mom's gesture, then he stiffened. He turned to Kayla with a scowl. She flinched, not sure why he looked ready to bite her head off. "What's wrong?"

"Nothing. Nothing at all," he muttered. He straightened to his full height and then smiled at her mom. "Why don't you go along ahead of us, Mrs. Moriarity. I just want a second with Kayla before we follow."

"Of course, dear. I'll see you in a few."

She practically skipped toward the corner where Kayla's dad sat, frowning at Cooper even from across the room. Cooper waved at him politely, then turned to Kayla. "At what point were you going to mention your father is the man I'm going to be working for?"

Chapter Eleven

Cooper couldn't believe it. The guy sitting in the corner was his new boss. What the hell were the chances of that happening? He bet Kayla knew. She always knew the answers to weird shit like that.

But she had failed to tell him about *this*.

Kayla blinked at him, then looked over at her father again. "I think you're mistaken. My father isn't in private security. He's a cop."

He dragged a hand through his hair. He hadn't been expecting this. And he didn't know if this fake relationship with Kayla would work *for* him or *against* him in this situation. "A cop that runs a private security firm?"

"No…he's just a cop." Kayla pursed her lips. "A homicide detective. I think you're looking at the wrong guy."

"Well, then, which one is your father?"

She pointed at the guy next to his new boss. "The one in the black suit and the green shirt."

Of *course* her father was the guy who looked as if he wanted to pummel Cooper into the ground for touching his baby girl. And of course her father would be a cop who probably had an arsenal of excellent ideas of how to properly dispose of a body.

"Who were you looking at?" she asked.

"The one in the grey and purple."

"Oh." She nodded. "That's Uncle Frankie. Well, we call him uncle, but he's just a family friend."

Cooper sighed. "He's the guy who hired me."

"Oh. Well, let's go say hi." She caught his hand and tugged him toward his employer and the man who looked as if he'd like nothing more than to kill him. "It'll be nice having a friendly face when you meet my dad. Trust me."

"What will your father say when—"

"I don't know. There's a sixty-three percent chance that this will backfire, but it's too late to back down now. They've both seen you and they know who you are. There's nothing to be done except to walk up and say hi."

"Shit." He dragged his hand down his face. He didn't like this, but she was right. He couldn't exactly tell them the truth, could he? "Fuck it. Let's go."

She nodded and they crossed the room to stand in front of Kayla's unfriendly looking father. "Dad, meet my boyfriend, Cooper Shillings." The smile on her face was forced, but hopefully only Cooper noticed that. "Cooper, this is my father, Greg Moriarity. And that's his best friend, Frankie Holt."

Cooper tensed but managed a smile. "Nice to meet you, Mr. Moriarity." He shook hands with her father. The man practically broke his fingers, but Cooper didn't flinch. "And nice seeing you again, Mr. Holt."

Mr. Holt shook his hand, his brow furrowed. "Cooper. I didn't know you were dating my niece."

Cooper forced a laugh. "And I didn't know my girlfriend was *your* niece."

"I'd imagine not." Mr. Holt didn't let go of his hand. "How does she feel about you leaving?"

"*She* is right here," Kayla said. "And I'm fine with it."

"Yes, sir, she is." Cooper extracted his fingers from the man's hold. "We have a great support system."

"Wait a second." Kayla's father watched him with narrowed eyes. "What's the position and where is it?"

"It's an overseas assignment." Mr. Holt sat back down and smoothed his suit jacket. "Mr. Shillings here used to be a Marine, and he's going back over with his team as a guard now. He leaves next week."

Cooper shifted on his feet. This was the complication Cooper had been trying to warn Kayla about. What would her father say about a boyfriend that was leaving her behind to go fight overseas? "Yes, I am."

Her dad narrowed his eyes on Cooper. "So, you get involved with my baby girl and then you leave?"

Cooper flinched. He didn't do that and never would. "Actually, sir, I—"

"Stop it, Dad," Kayla cut in with. "He's just doing his job. He's trying to protect the people fighting for his country. It's honorable and I'm proud of him." Kayla curled a hand around his biceps, surprising Cooper. "Don't you dare give him a hard time about that. You of all people should support him."

Mr. Holt cleared his throat. "We'll take good care of him,

Greg." He looked at Kayla. "I promise that much."

She nodded, but she looked a lot paler than she had before. "Thanks, Uncle Frankie." Then she faced her dad again. "Just so you know? I'm behind his decision one hundred percent. No odd numbers or decimal points."

Cooper glanced down at her, something warm taking over his heart. "Thanks, sweetheart. I support you, too."

"I know." She smiled up at him. "And you're welcome."

Her dad relaxed a little bit, his eyes still locked on Cooper and Kayla—watching the way the two of them were interacting. Something told Cooper her father saw way too much, but he nodded and gestured toward the empty seats at the table.

"Sit. Talk. Drink," her father said.

Kayla squeezed his arm again and sat down gracefully. She might not be used to this charade, but she was fucking good at it. The way she kept smiling with those bright blue eyes of hers shining up at him made him want to wrap her in his arms and hold her close all night long. Hell, maybe even longer.

"Sir, I'm very excited to meet you, just for the record. Kayla told me a lot about you," Cooper said, focusing on Kayla's father. "I'm honored to be here."

"Are you now?" He eyed Cooper, his voice clearly skeptical. "So, tell me more about yourself."

Cooper gripped his own knee under the table. "I was in the Marines, and I'm from Maine, near Kayla. I just recently got home after getting out, and now I'm about to make my next career move..." He broke off, smiled, and gestured toward Mr. Holt. "But you already heard that part earlier."

Mr. Holt laughed. "We've already completed the

background check, Greg. He's legit."

"I see." He tapped his fingers on the table. "Parents?"

"Still happily married and living in Maine."

"What do they do—or are they leaving the country, too?"

Kayla rolled her eyes. "*Dad.*"

"It's fine. I don't mind." Cooper smiled at Kayla, trying to show her that he didn't care about her father's curiosity. Because he didn't. He understood wanting to protect the people he cared about. It's what he wanted to do, too, overseas. "My father owns a private security firm, among other things, and my mother is an artist."

Mr. Holt perked up at that. "Your father owns a private security firm, but you're working for me?"

"Yes." Cooper shifted his weight and tugged on his collar, despite himself. "That's right, sir. I feel it's important for a man to make his own way. I don't want to get a position because of my last name."

Her father nodded and Cooper swore he saw something that wasn't hatred in the other man's stare. Maybe…respect? No. That couldn't be it. Maybe he just had something in his eye. "All right." He looked over Cooper's shoulder. "I'll see you two later, though. Max's family just got here, and I have to go say hi. Frankie? You coming?"

Mr. Holt stood. "Of course. I'll see you two later."

Cooper inclined his head, then watched as they left. "Well. That was interesting, to say the least."

"It went better than I thought it would." Kayla leaned her head on him. "You did good, by the way."

He kissed her temple. This snuggling thing didn't feel too bad. "It's the dimples. No one can resist the power."

"Not even my father," she said, laughter in her voice. She lifted her head and grinned at him. "Right?"

"Especially not your dad." He stood up, then held his arm out for her. "Ready to have a drink?"

"How about ten?"

He pretended to consider this. "I don't think that's a good idea. I'd hate to have to restock the bar."

"I'm not that bad." She swatted his arm, then curled her fingers around his biceps. "Let's do this."

He led her toward the bar, strangely content to have her at his side.

Chapter Twelve

The next hour flew by in a haze of introductions and mind-numbing craziness from everyone. Everyone wanted to know how they met. Wanted to know what Cooper did for a living. How long he was staying. Everyone wanted to know…well, everything. Everyone wanted to meet Cooper, and Kayla *wanted* everyone to meet Cooper.

Sure, she'd been hesitant about this at first, but he was such a great guy that the whole being her "boyfriend" thing came naturally to him. Sometimes even *she* forgot it was all an act. She wasn't sure what to make of that, exactly, but, hey, whatever.

It totally worked.

Even now, Cooper was surrounded by her female family members, and they all hung on every word he said. He had them all enamored, and he didn't even have to try. She couldn't believe it. His strong baritone voice cut through the space. "…and then the plane landed, and the rest is history."

"Wait, so you flew with her? That's how you two met?" her mom asked, her eyes wide. "How did *that* go?"

Susan leaned in. "And how did your not-even-there-yet relationship survive it?"

"Oh, I found her nervousness charming." Cooper threw his arm around Kayla's shoulders and smiled. "She needed a knight in shining armor, and I've always had a thing for a damsel in distress. We were the perfect fit."

Cue eye roll. "Yeah, we really were. Still are, somehow."

"Because we work," Cooper said, reaching out and cupping Kayla's cheek. His warm gaze stared down into hers, stealing her thoughts right out of her head. "*So* very well."

Even though she *knew* he was putting a show on for the women, she still had to catch her breath when he leaned in and kissed her sweetly. He looked at her as if she was the only thing that mattered to him. And it felt real—his lips on hers and the emotion behind them.

Man, he was good.

He had them all on puppet strings, and he was the puppeteer. If she wasn't careful, she'd be on a string, too. She pulled back, her cheeks burning. Cooper stared down at her, something unspoken and deep in his eyes.

Something she couldn't read. "Hey," she whispered.

"Hey," he said back, his gaze finally clearing. He noticed her family, then gave them a sheepish grin, "Oops. Forgot we had an audience."

"Keep him," her mom whispered. She turned her attention to everyone else. "All right. Enough bothering the lovebirds. It's time for me to go on stage, and then it'll be you, Kayla. Everyone, to your seats."

One by one, they all dispersed to their assigned seats and Cooper led her to the table next to her father. Her heart was still racing from the kiss he'd given her earlier, and her legs were a little bit wobbly. This was freaking ridiculous. She wasn't the type of girl to swoon over her man, and she wasn't about to start with a *fake* relationship of all things.

Sinking into her chair, she gulped down her cool water, not stopping until the glass was empty. God knew she needed all the help she could get in cooling the heck off.

"You all right over there?" Cooper asked, a brow up.

"Yeah, sure." She set down her glass, then pointed to his untouched drink. "You going to drink that?"

Cooper held his cup out to her. "It's all yours, sweetheart. Thirsty much?"

"God, yes." Snatching the glass out of his hand, she tipped it back and emptied it without a break. After she was finished, she swiped her hand across her wet lips. "Thank you."

His eyes on her mouth, he reached out and wiped away a drop she must have missed with his thumb. "You're very welcome."

She shivered, his thumb leaving a trail of fire in its wake. So much for cooling off. "Uh, I need to read over my speech one more time."

"Go ahead."

She pulled back. "You're touching me. I can't."

"You can't read while I'm touching you?" he asked, his voice light.

"Nope." She pulled the paper out of her purse with a trembling hand. "So hands off, mister."

He held them up in surrender. "Yes, ma'am."

She shot him one last look, then focused on the words she'd written instead of the man at her side. Somewhere in all the pretending and kisses, her body was forgetting that this was all for show. He didn't really love her, and she didn't love him, either. This was all fake.

Fake, fake, fake.

She needed to focus on something that wasn't pretend.

She lowered her head and checked him out from under her lashes. Thank God he'd packed a suit just in case he had a business meeting. He was so handsome in it…and the fabric grazed his whipcord lean body just right. What she was going to do with him once they got back to the hotel *definitely* wasn't fake.

The microphone crackled and Cooper jumped. He glanced over his shoulder then turned back to her. Tugging on his collar, he shifted in his seat and asked, "When do you go on?"

"I'm first, so in a couple of minutes." She peeked at him over the top of her paper. "You okay?"

"Yeah. Do you need a drink stronger than water before you get up there?" he asked, his voice tight. "A Xanax? Sex? Something to help you relax?"

A laugh bubbled out of her. "Uh, no thanks? I'm fine. I worked on this speech for months because I wanted it to be perfect. Susan deserves perfect." She shifted closer and squeezed his knee. "*You* look like you're about to panic, though. What's up?"

He averted his eyes. "I just don't like stages, is all."

She studied him closely. He wasn't kidding. He had sweat on his forehead and he looked ready to run for the door, and *he* wasn't even going up there. "Sweetie, you're not going up there. You'll be okay."

She had forgotten his fear of public speaking, or being on a stage. The fact that this big, strong man could be scared of something at all, let alone something so trivial, struck her as oddly cute. He seemed so invincible the rest of the time it made her want to hug him and kiss him now that he *wasn't*.

If anything, it made him hotter.

He swiped his forearm over his sweaty forehead. "I know. It's stupid, but I hate those things. And having the spotlight on you is just as bad. Everyone watches you."

"It won't come near you, don't worry. You can stay here. It'll give you a break from acting as if you love me. You've got to be sick of it already."

"I'm not, though." He met her eyes. "This isn't all an act, you know. Well, the love part is, but that's it. I *do* like you, and I like being with you. I'm having a lot of fun. If things were different and I wasn't leaving…" He shrugged. "Well, it doesn't matter. Because I am."

Kayla swallowed hard, her heart stuttering and then speeding up. He had to stop saying things like that, or she would want to spend more time with him, too. And that just wasn't possible. She didn't want a real relationship any more than he did. He was leaving. And she wanted to live her own life free of meddling family members and husbands trying to tell her what to do.

But then again…

No. No buts.

This was not real.

She shook her head. "Cooper…"

"I know. But when—" He cut himself off and glanced at the stage. Kayla waited, wanting to see what he would finish that sentence off with. Instead he said, "I think they want you to go up now. They're staring at us."

"Oh. Right." Kayla stood. It was probably better he didn't finish that thought anyway. "Wish me luck."

He tugged at his collar again. "Knock 'em dead."

Kayla made her way to the stage. Her mother stood next to the microphone, smiling at the crowd like some benevolent queen upon her subjects. The spotlight made her mother's diamond necklace sparkle, blinding everyone who watched.

Kayla closed the distance between them, smoothing her purple skirt as she walked. Her mom gestured her closer. "First on the roster, we have the maid of honor who is none other than my other wonderful daughter, Kayla."

Polite applause filled the room at the unnecessary introduction. Most of the people knew who she was, after all. Clearing her throat, Kayla stepped up to the microphone. "My little sister might be all grown up, and might be getting married in a few short days, but to me, she's still the little girl who used to keep me awake every night. She used to make me watch her until she fell asleep, so the monsters wouldn't come get her. She was sure if I stayed up and watched over her, nothing bad would happen.

"I don't know what I did to deserve such a vote of confidence from her, but I dutifully stayed awake and did what she asked. Sometimes when she couldn't fall asleep, we'd just talk. Usually it was a different topic, but at least once a week, before she drifted off to sleep, she would tell me about her wedding day. She would look like a princess, and everyone would cry as she walked down the aisle. Everyone would be watching her, unable to believe she could be so lucky as to catch the man of her dreams. And she was going to marry a man as wonderful as our daddy. "

Kayla had wanted that, too, at the time. So badly. She broke off, swallowing past the lump in her throat. *Pull it together. Don't buy into this emotional crap.*

She looked at Cooper. He nodded at her, smiling, and she felt better. "I think Susan made the right choice in Max because I can tell he loves her very much. Heck, he's been following her around since second grade. All you have to do is look at him when he thinks no one is watching, and you'll see it. I'm also quite sure when we all see her walking down the aisle Saturday, there will be tears in our eyes." She turned to her little sis, who was practically sparkling from happiness. Even the normally reserved Max was grinning ear-to-ear.

Family pressure and fake boyfriend drama aside, she was thrilled for both of them. It's why she'd concocted this lie in the first place—so the focus wouldn't be on when Kayla would find someone. Which, unfortunately, was exactly what had happened at Susan's bridal shower a while back. Now, people would be content that Kayla was happy, and all eyes would be where they belonged.

On her sister.

"I'm so thrilled for you, Susan, and I wish you nothing but happiness in life—but I'm positive you don't need any help from me anymore. I know you two will be together forever, and he'll be the one standing guard over you from now on."

She lifted the glass of champagne her mother handed her, smiling past her unshed tears. "To your happily ever after."

Susan stood and called out, "And to yours."

Kayla looked at Cooper...*again*. He still sat at their

table, watching her with a light in his eyes that literally took her breath away. For a second, and only a second, she let herself imagine a future with him.

And it looked good.

But then she shoved the happily-ever-after forever thought away and focused on what she could have.

The sex.

Her happily-ever-after for tonight.

Her mother came over, wiping the tears off her face hurriedly. "Thank you, sweetie." Her mother hugged her, sniffing loudly. She whispered, "That was perfect. I love you."

"Thank you," Kayla whispered back. "Love you, too."

"If I can pull myself together now..." Her mom turned to the crowd and laughed. Everyone joined in. "Everyone, let's show our appreciation for Kayla."

The room full of people clapped, and Kayla saw Cooper stand and clap, too. He made a face at her, something silly and so *him*. She grinned and rolled her eyes back at him. Then he burst into laughter.

God, he was hot when he did that.

She made her way down the stairs, and he came across the room. In the background, her mom talked about Susan and Max, but Kayla didn't hear a word. Cooper pulled her into his arms under the guise of a sweet hug for her family's benefit, but once he lowered his mouth to her ear, he said, "You did great. I promise a huge reward when we get back to the hotel."

Oh, God, yes please.

As happy as she was for her sister, and as much as she loved her family...

She wanted tonight to be over so she could collect.

Chapter Thirteen

Cooper closed the hotel door behind them, his eyes on Kayla. He watched her as she stepped out of her heels, wobbling a little bit as she did so. She looked so fucking pretty she stole his breath away, but he couldn't stop watching. She was addicting.

He should be exhausted. Should be ready to collapse.

God knew she'd kept him up all night last night.

But he wanted her again. They would only be together for a few days and he was determined to have her as much, and in as many ways, as possible within that short time. He crossed the room and swooped her into his arms. Then he lowered his head and kissed her, his tongue claiming hers. Walking across the room, he carried her to the bed and set her down on it.

Her slender leg curved at the knee, and he crept his hand up her skin. He spread her thighs as he nibbled her throat, his stomach clenching down hard when she moaned and scraped her nails down his back. "Fuck, you taste good."

He made quick work of removing his clothes and her dress, and then looked at her. Just looked. She was gorgeous. All pinks and creamy skin and perfection.

After a moment of hesitation, he closed his mouth around her nipple. She cried out and squirmed beneath him. Good. Desire formed a hard coil in his stomach and he slid his fingers along her pussy. His fingers were instantly drenched.

She flicked her tongue over his shoulder, then bit down. "God, I want you now."

"You want more? You want this?" He slipped a finger inside of her, rubbing against her clit as he did so. Silk. Pure silk. "Or do you want my cock inside of you?"

She lifted her hips, rolling them against him urgently. "I want it all," she breathed, her eyes drifting shut. "Give it all to me."

"You need more…" He sucked on her nipple and slid another finger inside of her, thrusting his hand hard. "… Patience."

Christ, she felt so damn good. His cock twitched, demanding to take the place of his fingers. But he wouldn't give in to that yet. He wouldn't give in until she was crying his name so loudly they woke up the entire fucking hotel.

He kissed a path down her stomach, his fingers still moving inside of her. She thrust her hips and buried her fingers in his hair as she tried to pull him closer.

"Cooper. Please."

He groaned, lowering his head even more. He nipped the skin right over the small patch of curls between her legs. Her abs clenched, and her grip on his head relaxed. But a second later, her fingers tightened and she was urging him lower.

Now *that*, he would happily give her.

He rolled his tongue over her clit, closing his eyes when she arched into him. Her thighs tightened around his head, squeezing and trembling at the same time. She was close already. He increased the pressure, slid his hands under her ass, and lifted her up. He traced his thumbs over the curve of her ass, sliding inwards as he ravaged her with his mouth. She tensed and screamed, her entire body going tight as her juices coated his tongue.

He pushed up off of her and stood, crossing the room to grab a condom. She started to roll over, but he stopped her. "Stay where you are. I'm not done tasting you yet."

Her eyes went wide and she fell back again, watching him as he walked. "Keep that up and I might want to keep you around even after the wedding," she teased, a seductive smile on her face.

Ha! As if she'd want to. Sex was one thing. But once she got to know him better, she'd see that he wasn't worth keeping around.

So he didn't bother to reply.

Instead, he grabbed a condom and rolled it onto his cock. Once properly sheathed, he came back and lowered himself on top of her, biting back a groan at how intoxicating her skin felt against his. Would he ever get enough of her? Of this?

He captured her lips and, without breaking contact, rolled over, bringing her with him so she was on top, straddling him.

Grabbing her hips, he guided her in a position guaranteed to make her come fast, and folded her legs around him. He pumped his hips up and cupped her breasts, going so deep inside her he wanted to shout.

The feel of her tight pussy around him and the vision of taking all of him in, her breasts bare and her eyes closed in ecstasy, almost pushed him over the edge.

As he pinched her nipples between his fingers, she flung her head back. Her long brown hair cascaded down her back as she rocked against him.

"Jesus," he groaned, lifting his hips again. "Come for me, Kayla."

She leaned forward until their chests touched and nipped at his lower lip. He cupped her ass and repositioned her so her clit rubbed against him with each thrust. Her inner muscles tightened around him even more, her breath coming hard.

She was close. So fucking close.

Rolling her onto her back, he slid her legs onto his shoulders and plunged inside her hard. Fast. His pulse raced and his cock begged for release, but he wouldn't allow himself to finish until she came one more time.

Just…one…more…time.

Her fingers fisted into the sheets and her back bowed, her whole body going tight. The walls of her pussy squeezed down on him as she came. Groaning, he pulled almost completely out then slammed back inside, his fingers flexing on her as he did so.

The room around him faded away, and the pleasure of his orgasm took over. Everything ceased to exist but this woman. This room. This moment.

Kayla.

He smoothed her hair off her face and placed a gentle

kiss on her lips. Her eyelids fluttered open, and she gripped his biceps. The way she looked up at him, her eyes soft and her lips swollen from his kisses, sent a pang of something unfamiliar to his heart.

If he didn't know better, he would swear it was something dangerously close to…*feeling*. Something more than attraction and lust. But that would be completely foolish under the circumstances. Whatever this warmth in his heart was, he had best terminate it with a kill shot. He was leaving soon.

He withdrew from her and pushed off of the bed in one motion. As he rolled off the condom, he headed toward the bathroom, needing a few moments of privacy before he faced her again. After brushing his teeth, he took a quick shower, hoping that would make him feel like himself again.

The Cooper from a few days ago.

But it didn't work. She was on his mind the whole time.

The most he could hope for was that she hadn't seen the vulnerability he was feeling, or sensed the tenderness in his heart that snuck up on him like a ninja. He couldn't afford to be distracted by any doubts as to his goals, nor could he afford to want more than a few days with Kayla.

He had a lot of mistakes to make up for, and his first step to that end had been getting the job with Frankie Holt. The second would be going overseas and protecting his men. With this job, he would be protecting the same team he had let down before. The men he'd failed. He would keep them safe, even though he hadn't kept Josh safe.

He owed it to them. Hell, to himself, too.

As he dried off, he studied himself in the mirror. Same dark circles. Same haunted eyes. Same guilty conscience.

Nothing had changed in the last day, despite the short-term happiness he'd found in Kayla's arms. Good. The guilt was his constant companion, and he needed it with him.

Keeping him focused.

Chapter Fourteen

By the time Cooper came back from his shower, Kayla was a nervous wreck. He'd seemed...*done.* As if he wanted to leave her. And then...he had.

He'd walked away without a word.

The bathroom door opened, and he came out. He didn't have a towel on, but he was scrubbing his head with the one he'd used to dry off with. He was gloriously naked and the black tribal tattoos on his chest danced with every movement he made.

He came to his side of the bed, then lay down beside her.

"Hey," she said softly.

He turned his head toward her. His green eyes sucked her in, like usual. "Hey yourself."

"You okay?"

"Yep." He looked at her with a wrinkled brow. "After what we just did, why *wouldn't* I be okay?"

"I don't know. I just got a feeling—"

He rolled his eyes and laughed, but it sounded a little forced. "This isn't a real relationship. You don't have to worry about my mood swings. I'm fine."

"But we should talk about whatever you're thinking. I know there's something on your mind, so don't pretend otherwise."

"You're right. There is. But that's where it's staying—in the privacy of my own mind." He turned over and cupped her cheek. "But if you want to talk about feelings, let's do this. Tell me. Why do you feel the need to lie to your parents?"

She blinked at him, totally confused. "What do you mean?"

"They love you. Even I can see that. I think if you just explained that you're perfectly happy single, or that you just haven't met the right guy, they'd back off. Have you ever considered just talking it out with them?"

She pulled away from him. Was he trying to lecture her about her parents? Please. She knew them much better than he did, thank you very much.

She cleared her throat. "You know what? You're right. Let's not do this."

"Oh, so now you're on board with the not talking thing?" He rolled to his back, folded his arms behind his head and smirked. "Typical fake girlfriend behavior."

Anger surged through her, red hot. "This relationship might not be real, but I *will* kick my fake boyfriend's ass. Consider yourself warned."

His smirk widened, which only pissed her off even more. "Consider me scared, if it makes you happy."

"*Cooper.*" She curled her hands into fists. Where the heck had this fight even come from? Oh. Right. She'd asked him about his feelings. How stupid of her. "This conversation is over."

"Fine." He turned his head toward her. "But have you ever considered it's in your mind—all these troubles you think exist with your family?"

She tilted her chin up. "Are they in yours?"

"What do you mean?"

"Maybe your advice applies to your *own* dad. Maybe if you talked it out with him, you'd see he loves you and isn't trying to hand you something on a platter. That he isn't trying to offer you a consolation prize for disappointing him. Maybe he just wants to give his life's work to his son, crazy as it might sound."

"That advice does not apply to me," he said through clenched teeth. "I simply want an even playing field. I'm not lying or making up a fake life to make him happy. I'm not the one being close-minded about reality."

She flinched. He wanted to attack her where she was weak? Bullshit. "Why does the ground always have to be *even*? What's so wrong with using something to your advantage if it's presented to you?"

"It's just not how I roll."

"Yeah." She studied him, taking in the stubborn cut of his jaw. "I got that loud and clear."

His nostrils flared. "Let me guess. You think it's stupid and that I should just 'talk it out' with him? As if that will fix the problem of me not taking something I didn't earn out of principle?"

"Who says you didn't earn it?"

He tugged the blankets up over his body. "Being my father's son isn't a fucking job qualification, Kayla. And I have other debts to pay. Now drop it."

"Maybe he's offering the position to you because he feels you're the right man for it. Maybe he admires your work and dedication. Did *you* ever think of *that*?"

He glared at her and rolled over, giving her his back. "My father is *not* your father. Now go the fuck to sleep, *sweetheart*."

She punched her pillow, fidgeting to get comfortable. "Sleep tight and secure in your ignorance, *darling*."

He stiffened even more but didn't rise to the bait. When she realized he wasn't going to fight back, she rolled over and glared at the dark room. She'd been right to avoid love and commitment like the plague.

Even fake relationships sucked ass.

• • •

The next morning, Kayla lay in the bed, staring at the sunlight forming shapes and shadows on the hotel ceiling. Last night had been…weird. The fight had been way too intense and… well, *real*.

Since when did fake relationships start having real fights?

Maybe they were getting too caught up in the charade and just needed to laugh it off this morning. Do a reset or something. She rolled over and rested her hands under her cheek, watching him as he slept. He looked so peaceful.

She knew he wasn't.

He was haunted by his memories, and there was nothing she or anyone could do to help him. He had to let go of those nightmares all by himself. And he had to forgive himself. She only wished she could make it easier. They'd come together because he'd been trying to save her.

But he needed saving, too.

His lids fluttered open, and his bright green gaze met hers. His light brown hair was sloppy and standing up on ends, and he had a major five o'clock shadow going on. His tattoos stood out against the white sheets on the bed. He was even super-hot first thing in the morning.

Not. Fair.

"Good morning," she said, smiling at him. "So, that fight was…interesting, huh?"

His lips twitched. "To say the least."

"Why were we arguing when this whole boyfriend-girlfriend thing is fake, anyway?"

"I have no clue." He curled his arm around her waist and rolled her underneath him, his eyes back to being warm and carefree. Thank God. "But you know the best part about fake fighting?"

She wrapped her arms around his neck. "What would that be?"

"The real make-up sex you have afterwards." He grabbed her leg and bent it at the knee, his cock brushing against her with deadly precision. "You ready to make up, sweetheart?"

"God, yes."

She tugged him down and kissed him, her tongue finding his. His hands roamed everywhere, exploring her body as if he was memorizing every single curve. She wrapped her legs around his waist and gripped his muscled back. Man, she loved how hard he felt.

How invincible he seemed.

She had a feeling he liked showing that image to the world…even if it wasn't entirely accurate.

He nibbled his way down her neck, her chest, and then clamped on to her nipple. He sucked with the perfect amount of pressure, as he ran his fingers down her stomach and over her hip.

Her insides quivered. Begged for more of it—lots more. And he gave it to her. He rolled her over onto her stomach, then slid lower, his hard body moving down hers with teasing slowness. She curled her fingers into the mattress and held her breath. He kissed down her spine, and then over the curve of her butt.

And then, oh God, then he slipped between her legs and lifted her hips so he could go down on her from behind. She cried out and buried her face in the pillow, loving the way he made her feel. It was such a vulnerable position, but with Cooper?

There were no words.

His fingers flexed on her hips, and then dug in just enough to hurt a little bit. She whimpered and pressed back against him, so close. And then she soared over the edge, her whole body going tense.

She felt him pull away from her and she heard the sound of a condom wrapper ripping. And when he positioned himself behind her, lifting her on to her knees, she held her breath and waited. Waited for him to rock her world all over again.

He didn't disappoint.

He surged inside of her, burying himself completely. She pressed even closer to him, loving how much he filled her. And then all hell broke loose, because he was moving inside of her and need took over, not allowing for anything besides him.

And this.

Her entire body tightened and grew intensely sensitive, and he moved inside her smooth and hard. She came again. Explosively. Unexpectedly. No one else had ever given her multiple orgasms like this. After a few moments, she crashed back down to earth in time to feel him come inside of her. He gripped her ass so tight it hurt, but then he collapsed on top of her with a shudder.

And it was then...right then...that she realized something crazy. This wasn't strictly fun, carefree sex anymore. He made her feel better, in the bed and out of it. He made her *happy*. Like, long-term-share-my-hopes-and-dreams kind of happy.

What the heck was she supposed to do with that?

They both rolled to their sides so that they faced one another. He had a smile on those lips she loved so much—full dimples and all. "That was the best fake-make up sex *ever*."

"Agreed," she said, keeping her tone light even though she was panicking inside.

He reached out and toyed with her hair. "If that's what I get for fake-fighting with you, then I just might love fighting with you from now on. Want to go again?"

There was that word again. *Love*. That word on his lips did strange things to her heart. Like making her want to hear it for real.

Oh, God. Had she really just thought that? Please, no.

"Kayla? You okay?" he asked, his brow furrowed.

"Uh, yeah." She forced a laugh. It sounded maniacal. "Why would you ask?"

"Because you've been quiet for three minutes." He ran a finger down her cheek. "Just...staring at me."

Her cheeks went red hot, but she forced a smile. He wouldn't know. He could never know. "Well, in my defense you're quite fun to look at."

"Yeah?" His lips twitched. "Back 'atcha, sweetheart."

"Gee, thanks."

"So, what's on the agenda today?" He lightly ran his hands up and down her sides, making chills dance over her body. "Are we busy?"

"Um, let's see…the family dinner is tonight, but the rest of the morning and afternoon are wide open. Susan wanted to be able to sleep in and relax the day before the wedding, instead of all that rehearsal dinner crap the night before. That's why we did it last night instead of tonight."

"So we have a few hours before we report for duty?"

"Yep." She rolled to her feet and headed for the bathroom. "Why? What do you want to do?"

He followed her, then leaned against the doorjamb, right next to the spot where she'd watched him take her in front of the mirror. Had that been only yesterday?

"How about if you show me the town? Your old haunts, or maybe your old school?"

She cringed. She'd hated high school…falling perfectly into the majority statistic. About seventy-three percent of kids hated high school. The only ones that didn't were the cool kids. "Hmmm… That sounds awfully *real*. Why would you want to see my old school?"

"Because you went there," he said, his voice soft. "Please?"

"Cooper…" she said, drifting off. And when he looked at her, all warm eyes and hard abs and sexy lips…who was she to say no? "All right. We'll do it."

"Fuck yeah. Let's do this," he quipped.

She closed her eyes for a second at the onslaught of feelings those words brought about. And then she sucked it the hell up and got in the shower.

Wondering how she was going to get him out of her life now that she'd already let him in.

Chapter Fifteen

The tall high school rose above them, extending into the overcast sky. What had started out as a sunny, bright day had quickly changed over to fog and drear. If he wasn't mistaken, they were in for a storm. A big one. He wondered what Susan would think about that. She'd probably been hoping for clear skies — not clouds and downpours.

But hadn't he heard someone say that rain was good luck for a wedding?

"What are the odds for bad weather tomorrow?" he asked, turning to Kayla. "You should know, right?"

She blinked at him. "Um, not really. I'm an actuary, not a weatherman."

"Is there a difference?" He wrapped her hand in his, tugging her around the back of the building. "Both look at the facts and spew out statistics at the general population, right?"

"Well when you put it that way…" She grinned and looked

up at the sky. Her graceful neck arched just right, and it made him pause. Since when had he been enthralled by a woman's neck, for fuck's sakes?

"I'm waiting."

"I know. I'm *thinking*." She shot him an annoyed look. "I'll put it at a fifty percent chance of rain."

"See? You even sound like a real weatherman."

She rolled her eyes. "It's okay. Rain is good luck for a wedding, contrary to popular belief. So it's a good thing."

"I thought I heard that somewhere." He led her toward the football field in the back. "So, tell me the truth. Were you on that field kicking your legs up and shaking your ass for all of the boys?"

She frowned at the field. "Not even close."

"Really? With that ass," he palmed her backside through the jeans, "and with that body," he trailed his fingers over her hips. He loved the way they curved so gracefully. "I'd have put my money on you being a cheerleader. Maybe even chief cheerleader."

"Well, you would have lost." She gave him a small smile. "Sadly, I was pretty much the furthest thing from a cheerleader."

"Hmm." He tapped a finger on his chin. "The jock?"

"*Puh-lease*."

"The math-a-lete?"

"Closer." She headed toward the field, her gaze on the bleachers. "I did like numbers, but that's not a shock, I'm sure."

"All right. I give up. What were you?"

She sighed. "I was in the five percent of the adolescent population that stayed in orchestra throughout high school."

He almost laughed, but didn't. He thought back on their time together. She had a habit of tapping her fingers when she was nervous or irritated. And for some reason, he thought for sure she must play the violin. He had no idea why. It was just a hunch, so he went with it. "Violin?"

"Yep." She smiled, but the smile looked sad. "I liked the music. And liked being in the orchestra. My part was always so clearly laid out. I knew exactly where I was seated and when to come in. It was comforting to a person like me."

"I can see that about you. Do you still play?"

"Sometimes." She shrugged. "I do it when I'm stressed out or thinking. But I miss being in an actual orchestra. It's the one place where I felt like I belonged. You know what I mean?"

He studied her. He might not have been a nerd in high school, but he'd never felt as if he belonged anywhere back then. Had never found his home, so to speak. Being a military brat, he'd never settled down long enough to really find a close group of friends or colleagues. Not until the military, when he forged some strong relationships with the guys around him. So he got what she meant way too well. He liked being needed. Liked helping others. But besides that… what did he have now?

Nothing. That's what.

He was tempted to make a joke and laugh off the moment. Make light of the fact that she'd shared something about herself she probably didn't tell many people. It's what he normally did. It was *him*. But he couldn't do it. Instead he cupped her cheek and ran his thumb over her lower lip. "I do know what you mean about belonging. But honestly? I don't think I've ever found that security."

She blinked up at him. "You have your career. Your men."

"Yeah, but do I belong there? Do I feel at peace?" He shrugged, feeling restless. "I don't think I could say that. I've never lost myself in something or someone so completely that everything else just faded away."

Not until you.

He immediately shook the thought from his head.

She snorted. "I find that hard to believe. You seem to know exactly where you're going and what you're doing at every point in time." She headed for the bleachers, her hand still holding his. "I know you like helping people, and I know you have a life plan that you stick to—and that's half of what you need to get where you want to be in life. You know what you want, and you go get it. That's awesome."

"What's the other half?"

"Sheer, stubborn determination to win." She eyed him, a smile playing on her lips. "I think you've got that down, too."

He laughed. "You think?"

"Oh yeah." She opened the gate and walked into the stands. He couldn't believe it wasn't locked, but maybe they didn't worry about that in North Carolina. "You've definitely got the stubborn part down to an art form. I mean, look at the way you took over and demanded to be my fake boyfriend? If that isn't sheer determination, then I don't know what is."

"Nah. I just wanted to get in your pants."

"Well, you succeeded." She grinned up at him.

"That's something I've always been pretty confident in," he joked, tightening his fingers on hers. "My ability to woo a woman."

"Yeah, I can see why."

"Though, I never went to the extremes with anyone else that I went to with you." He roamed his gaze over her. She wore a grey wool jacket, a pair of jeans, and a white knit hat. Her cheeks were flushed from the cold, and she looked so damn pretty it hurt.

She chuckled. He expected her to say something sentimental or sweet, but she turned away, her cheeks going even redder. "You didn't tell me who you were in high school yet."

He blinked at the change of subject. "Uh...why don't you guess?"

"Guess?" She strolled toward the area where the team sits when they're not on the field. "I have a ninety-four percent chance of getting it right, based on what I know about you."

He raised a brow. "Sounds as if you like those odds."

"I do."

"Enough to bet on it?"

"Hmmm…" She paused, as if she was worried she might be wrong. "What are we talking here? Money? Sexual favors?"

He scanned the surrounding area. There were no cameras, and they were definitely the only ones here. "If you're wrong, you have to do any sexual favor I ask for."

She laughed. "That's all?"

"Yep." He gestured toward the field. "Right here. Right now."

She sucked in a deep breath, then blew it out. He could almost make out her breath in the cold air. "Seriously?"

"What's the matter?" He spun her until her back rested against the chain link fence, then grabbed both her hands. He lifted them so they pressed against the metal on either side of her head. "Are you too scared your calculations are off?"

"God, no." She bit down on her lip, her gaze on his mouth. "Fine, but I pick the favor."

He groaned. "Deal. Go ahead and guess already." He nibbled on the side of her neck. "Take all the facts you know about me and tell me what I was like in high school."

When he lowered his head and nipped the spot where her shoulder and neck met, she groaned and arched her back. "You're very take charge, and you came from a military family, so you probably moved around a lot. It wouldn't have given you a good chance to develop the team camaraderie that most sports need to flow nicely, and you were always the new kid, so I'm guessing you weren't in any sports. You don't strike me as the musical type, so I'm thinking…"

When she didn't finish, he cocked a brow. "Yeah?"

"You were the guy who kept to the edge of the crowd, didn't have any activities he excelled at, even though you were smart. I'd say you were into art and a loner. Maybe even a skater boy."

He shook his head. "Wrong."

"Not possible." She narrowed her eyes on him. "You're lying."

He laughed. "I'm not lying. Your odds were off, and you lost."

"Impossible," she said, her lips pressed tight. "What were you, then?"

"Hmm."

He lowered his mouth to hers. But he didn't kiss her. He just hovered there, enjoying the moment. Her hands curled into fists, but she didn't fight his hold. "Tell me," she demanded.

"I was the quarterback—the guy chasing down the cheerleaders. And they chased me, too."

"No way. That's not possible."

He laughed. "I assure you it's true."

"If you were always moving around, how did you gain that position without knowing the coaches? The rest of the team?"

"I was just that good."

She turned her head, a challenging light in her eyes. "Prove it."

"And how do you propose I do that?" He looked at the area she'd been looking at. There was an errant football under the corner of the bleachers. "Ah. I see now."

"If you can throw a ball and impress me? *Then* you win."

"I already won." He lowered his head towards her. "Be warned: I will be collecting my prize as soon as I throw that ball."

She smirked up at him. "Consider me scared."

He laughed at how she'd turned his words from last night back on him. He pushed off the fence, releasing her in the process, and then made his way over to the football. It had been years since he threw one with any seriousness besides fucking around in the desert, but he should still be able to prove he had skills.

Or that he'd *had* skills, anyway.

"We'll go mid-field, and then I'll throw it as hard as I can. Deal?"

"Deal." She started running toward the field. "Let's go, slow-poke!"

He shook his head at her silliness, and then easily caught

up to her. Hell, he could have blown past her, but what fun would that have been? By the time they made it to midfield, she was out of breath and he was laughing.

"All right." She bent over and rested her hand on her knees. "Impress me, quarterback boy."

He grinned. "Done."

"Wait," she called out, holding a hand up. "You need a kiss for good luck."

She straightened and then threw herself against him, kissing him full on the mouth, her arms snaking around his neck. He fumbled the ball as he wrapped his arms around her, hauling her close. Fuck football. He'd rather be playing with her.

But she broke away and danced out of his reach. "Go for it."

He took a deep breath, picked up the ball, and gave himself a second to re-center his bearings. Once he had it all figured out, he positioned himself, eyed the wind, and then cranked back before letting loose. The ball arced across the field with a perfect spiral, then hit the ground and bounced a bit before landing a little bit in front of the ten yard line.

He turned to her with a raised brow, and she looked back at him with her mouth parted. "Do you believe me now?" he asked.

"Yep," she sighed. "Damn you."

"I *told* you."

"Yeah, yeah." She started for the enclosed team stands. She crooked her finger at him, grinning as she walked backwards. "Let's go, lover boy."

He followed her, his hands shoved in his pockets. By the time they made it to the spot they'd been in earlier, he was lost in her. Mesmerized by the swing of her hips. The way her hair swayed with each step. Hell, with everything about her.

He had to reel it in. Now.

She turned and curled her hands around his neck. "Time for me to pay up. And I know just the way to do it."

He lowered his mouth to hers, kissing her as if his life depended on it. And, hell, right now it kind of felt like it *did*. And he was dying to know how she'd pay her debt.

She stepped closer, her hand dipping between their bodies to cup his cock. He groaned into her mouth, need coursing through his veins. She squeezed him, her fingers moving over him, and then she raised her hand, gripping his waistband tight.

When she slipped the button out of the loophole, he broke off the kiss. As much as he wanted to do this, he couldn't make her do something so private in such a public place. "You don't have to. I was just fucking around with you."

"Which is exactly what I'm trying to do with you."

She grabbed his hand and tugged him into the corner by the wall. As far as secure places in public went…this was as good as it got. No one would even know they were here unless they came around the corner and into the same area. Chances were they were safe.

But what if he was wrong?

She undid his button, then slowly unzipped his pants. Then knelt on the cement. The sight of her on her knees at his feet pushed him over the moral ledge. *Fuck it*. They were doing this.

She tugged his pants and boxers down, and he sucked in a deep breath at the frigid air hitting his cock. But then her mouth closed around him, and he forgot all about the cold and just focused on her. On what she made him feel. She sucked him in deep, her tongue rolling over the head, and he closed his eyes tight.

Holy fucking shit, she was incredible. Her hand curled around the back of his ass, holding him still, and she went down on him right here. Right now.

His entire body pulsed with the pleasure she gave him. His balls went tight and his stomach clenched, making him want to groan out loud. Kayla was amazing in every way. The fact that she was willing to do this—in public!—drove him fucking insane.

Then again, between the plane and the rental car lot, they'd done *lots* of things in public. He'd been told women like her existed. Women who were kind and funny and wild in bed. He hadn't believed it until now. Now he knew differently.

The perfect woman *did* exist—and her name was Kayla.

He clenched his jaw and watched her through his lowered lids. Seeing her on her knees in front of him, her mouth slowly taking him deeper and deeper until he was completely inside of her, sent him over the edge. She moaned, and he knew he was done.

He buried his hands in her hair and tried to tug her off. "I'm going to come. You need to stop."

She slapped his hands away and sucked harder. He tried to hold off. Tried to wait. But this was *her*, and he couldn't hold back. She was too damned amazing. He closed his eyes and arched into her mouth once, twice, then he exploded. She sucked harder, swallowing every drop. Then she let go of him inch by agonizing inch, her mouth slowly releasing him.

As she stood, she swiped a hand over her mouth, and then she tugged his boxers up. He reached down and quickly adjusted his pants, and within seconds, it was as if nothing had even happened.

They were both clothed and just standing there.

"Jesus, Kayla." He sagged against the wall of the cement wall. "Now it's your turn."

He reached for her, but she skirted out of his reach. "Nope. I don't get a turn. I lost fair and square—but you can make it up to me tonight, if you want."

"I don't care if you lost." He stalked after her. "I don't leave my women wanting, so get your ass back here."

Laughing, she backed up, the wind whipping her hair all about. "You sounded like a pimp just then. Just so you know."

"Gee, thanks." His response only made her laugh harder.

She glanced over her shoulder. "Let's go lay down on the field. I always wanted to lie in the middle and look up at the sky."

That made no sense. "Why would you want to do that? The ground is probably freezing."

She shrugged and walked backwards toward the field, a big smile on her face. "You coming?"

His breath lodged in his throat, and then he followed her. He had a habit of doing that. Following her around. If he was a lesser man, it just might bother him.

But he wasn't, and it didn't. And they might not have long together—only one more day, really—but until he walked away?

He'd be at her side, no holds barred.

Chapter Sixteen

Kayla flopped over in the middle of the field flat on her back and stared up at the clouds. It was going to rain any second now, but she couldn't bring herself to care. All day long, she and Cooper had been laughing and having fun.

Yet that happiness was overshadowed by the fact that he was leaving. She wasn't going to pretend otherwise. She liked him, and she couldn't help but wonder if they could become something real—more real than stolen moments and a fake relationship—if only they had more time together.

She'd always doubted there was someone out there that would make her want to settle down. To try a traditional relationship. But Cooper had made her reconsider her ways. He'd said he didn't want to leave a girl behind…but could she change his mind?

And if she could, was she really okay with being that girl left behind?

He lay down beside her. Their heads were side by side,

so she rolled hers to the left to face him. He was watching her intently, seeming to be as contemplative as she was. Was he thinking the same thing?

Did he not want to say good-bye, either?

He cupped the back of her head and kissed her, sweet and tender. She let her eyes drift shut, enjoying the moment. He ended it way too soon, pulling back and watching her with his warm green eyes. "We have to be at your parents' house in an hour."

"I know."

Then out of the blue, he asked, "If you could go anywhere at Christmas time—if money was no object—where would you go? Think about it before answering."

She hesitated. She'd never really thought about it before. Had been too busy visiting family and all that, but if she had the choice? "Why Christmas time?"

"The cities are always all lit up and decorated." He shrugged. "Seemed as good a time as any."

"Oh." She thought on it. "England. I've never been there, but Christmas time seems like a good time to go."

He laughed lightly. "You realize you'd have to fly. Like, I think it's safe to say you'd have a one hundred percent chance of flying."

"Nothing is one hundred percent." She met his eyes. "Like, ever. It's not a realistic number."

"I think *that* is," he said dryly.

"By the time I actually get to go? Who knows, there could be a new way. Teleporting or something. Or maybe even a good old fashioned ocean liner cruise." She shot him a grin. "Like I said. Nothing is one hundred percent."

"You told your dad that you were behind me one

hundred percent," he pointed out.

"Yeah, but I was just playing the part." She pursed her lips. "What about you? Where would you go?"

He shrugged. "I'd go somewhere warm. The Caribbean, maybe."

"Mm. That sounds nice, too. Blue water. Warm sand."

"Indeed," he said, his voice soft.

They both fell silent. She looked back up at the sky, watching the clouds. She'd swear the one above their heads looked like a heart.

Seriously, a heart.

What the hell had happened to her lately? She pictured her sister from last night, glowing with happiness as Max kissed her on the stage. They looked so happy. So normal. Did she really want that all of a sudden? It seemed too fast. Too much.

Cooper interrupted her thoughts. "What do you see up there? You look really focused on something."

She sighed. "A heart."

"Hm. I don't see it. Maybe if I…" He turned his head to the left, and then to the right. "Nope. I still just see a cloud."

She smacked him. He dodged out of the way even though he was flat on his back. She'd been caught thinking about her sister's marriage and seeing hearts in the sky.

Yep. There was something wrong with her.

"They look so happy, don't they?"

"The clouds?" He stared up at the sky with a wrinkled brow.

"No, my sister and Max."

"Hmmm. I guess so. People in love usually look happy, though."

"You think?" She turned to him. "I always thought they looked trapped."

A laugh escaped him. "Well, maybe some of them feel that way. I bet you have a statistic for that."

"Of course." She thought about it. "I'd say about fifty-seven percent are trapped, and forty-three percent are either ignorant of the fact that they feel trapped or genuinely happy."

He shook his head and then rolled it to the side, studying her. It made her wonder what he saw when he looked at her like that. As if she was a puzzle he couldn't quite figure out. Which was silly, really. She was easy to read. Too easy.

"I think you're pretty skeptical." He reached over his head and caught her hand. "I don't know what real love feels like, but if it feels as good as laying in an open field with you, it must be pretty fucking nice."

Her heart skipped a beat. Why did he say that? He was right, damn it all to hell and back. This did feel good. "What would your mom do if she saw us right now?"

"She wouldn't believe I was on a football field, holding hands with a woman instead of throwing a ball. Come to think of it, my father wouldn't believe it, either. He isn't one for relaxing and enjoying life. He's always working. Always has a plan. I probably get that from him."

She pursed her lips. "Tell me more about them."

"My mom is short but fiery as hell. She could swoop into a football locker room and scare the running back into submission with nothing more than a word." He snorted. "I've seen it happen, so I'm not exaggerating."

"I think I'd like her."

"I'm sure you would—and she'd love you, too."

Kayla wished she could have met her. Cooper knew her family, but she'd never get to meet his. "And your dad?"

"He's a hard-ass who doesn't allow any weakness of any sort." His voice went stiff and so did his body. "He loves me, and I know he does. But as his only son, I'm expected to lead the same life he did. Get married. Have babies. Run a business. Fight a war." He shrugged. "Anything short of that is a failure in his eyes."

"Sounds like my dad, but with slightly different goals. They both seem to think they know what is best for us."

He studied her. "Yeah, I guess they do."

"He's got to be happy with your career move now— even if it's not at the company of his choice."

"He's not." He rubbed the back of his neck.

She shifted slightly so she was more on her side than on her back. "Did you say you leave on Tuesday? I forget."

"Yeah, Tuesday." His fingers flexed on hers, and he ran his thumb over the back of her hand. "It's the right thing to do, you know."

"You like to be needed, don't you?"

His thumb stilled. "What do you mean?"

"You like when you're needed." She rolled onto her side, watching him closely. He was staring up at the sky. "It's not a bad thing. You just seem to thrive off of being *that guy*. It's why you swooped in and rescued me on that plane, and it's why you're still here. I'd bet it's why you're going back overseas, too. They need you—and you need them to need you."

"I…" He cleared his throat. "I guess so. Maybe. I suppose I have a pattern of liking to feel as if I'm accomplishing something. Shit, I don't know."

"*I* do." She cupped his cheek with her palm, running her thumb over his jaw. "I also know you're running from shadows that have haunted you since the war, and I know you think you're not a good man. I'm guessing you lost someone close to you, and you feel you're to blame. Maybe you even think it's solely on your shoulders. But you're one of the best men I know, and I hope you get to stop running soon."

He sat up and rested his forearms on his knees. "Anyone ever tell you that you read people a little too well?"

"Maybe."

He ran his hand through his mussed hair. "It's really ironic, considering you can't read your own parents."

She rolled to her feet and looked down at him, struggling to control her temper. "Let's not do this again, please? Fake relationship. No fighting. We agreed."

"Yeah, I know we did. I'm done. I just thought we were sharing deep dark secrets or some shit like that. Or was it only me?"

"Cooper..."

"I know." He stood, too, and dusted off his jeans. "Don't worry. I know. But before we go back to pretending we didn't make this thing between us too serious for a minute or two... Kayla?"

"Yeah?"

"Thank you for this weekend," he said softly. "Being with you...well, it's been a long time since I let myself relax. Laugh. It's been fun."

Her heart twisted. "No, thank *you*. You've...you restored my hope in men. Hell, humanity in general. You're a really special person, Cooper Shillings. Don't you dare forget it after you walk away, when I'm not here to remind you."

He swallowed hard and nodded. Then he held his hand out for hers. She should tell him that no one was watching so he didn't have to pretend. But she wanted to hold on to him. She wished she could say that they were still pretending when they did intimate things when no one was watching…

But she couldn't.

• • •

Cooper watched Kayla laugh with her parents from across the room. She'd gone to get them both drinks, so he was alone for the first time since they'd talked this afternoon. Opened up.

She knew things about him he hadn't even realized himself.

He hadn't said a word to her about losing someone in the war, yet she'd correctly reached that conclusion. What else did she know about him that he didn't want her to figure out? It's not as if she needed to be familiar with everything about him in this short-term deal they had going on. After tomorrow, he would walk away from her, and then they would be done.

Over. Finished. Never to speak again. No more communication meant no more pressure about opening up about Josh. About making amends with his father.

She might want to keep in touch via email or some shit like that, but if she asked? He'd tell her no. She didn't need to be worrying about him—and she didn't need to be sad if he died. She needed to move on. Laugh. Live. Have fun. Be free. Find new people to quote all of her random statistics to. They needed a clean cut. Fast, hard, and painful. Like ripping off a Band-Aid. Then she'd get over it quicker. Over him...if she even needed to get over him in the first place. Maybe he was the only one who had budding feelings that didn't belong. Maybe he was the only one left wanting more.

It didn't matter. He wouldn't get more.

And he was fine with that. Fucking fine.

He couldn't let her in. Wouldn't risk losing someone close to him again. Even now, he could close his eyes and see the same fucking thing happening all over again, as if he was reliving it in real time.

The sweltering hot sun. The nonexistent wind. And the smile on Josh's face...

Right until it got blown the fuck off by an IED.

He could even smell the blood and charred flesh of his best friend. Feel the way his heart raced as he sprinted down the hill, trying to get to him. To save him. But he'd been too late.

It had been his fault Josh was dead. Josh and the others. He was the one on lookout, the one supposed to keep them all safe. But he never saw the ambush coming, hadn't been able to save Josh.

Hadn't been able to save anyone.

They needed him to do better, and he would. But he wouldn't do it with a girl at home. His focus would be entirely on the platoon.

"You look awfully pensive for a pre-wedding dinner," Mr. Moriarity said, sinking down on the couch beside Cooper. He handed off a glass of scotch, then settled back against the pillows with his own drink. "What's going on?"

Cooper shifted in his seat and straightened his back.

Maybe it was old-fashioned, but he couldn't slouch in front of his elders. "I was just thinking about next week, sir."

He didn't know why he told him the truth. He should have lied and said he was admiring the beauty of the moment or some shit like that. But he'd already lied to the man about being in love with his daughter. Wasn't that enough?

"Your departure?" her father asked, his tone somber.

"Yeah. It's fast approaching."

Cooper looked at Kayla. She was laughing with Susan, and her mother watched them both with such love that Cooper wanted to take a picture and shove it under Kayla's nose. They obviously adored her, and if she just explained she didn't want a man in her life—that it hurt her when they pressured her to conform to their idea of what her life should be, rather than accepting her for who she is—they would get it. He didn't doubt that. It might take some time for her family to adjust, but they'd get there.

"You really love her, don't you?" her dad asked. "I can see it in your eyes."

Cooper swallowed a sip of whiskey and almost choked on his drink, unsure of what exactly to say to that question. "She's very special, sir," he offered.

That, at least, was the truth.

"You've got that right." Her father watched Kayla, a soft smile on his lips. "Are you upset you're leaving her?"

"Yes, sir. Very much."

That was true, too.

"A lot of men don't start relationships before they leave for that reason," Mr. Moriarity said. "You seem like the type of man who wouldn't want to put a woman through that. I had breakfast with Frankie this morning, and we were discussing you. I'm sorry about your best friend, by the way."

Cooper stiffened. "You know about that?"

"I do. I like to know what my daughter has gotten herself into. And I'm not going to apologize for that." He lifted the glass to his lips and took a gulp. "I like what I see, Cooper. You seem like a good guy, which is why I'm surprised you started up a relationship shortly before leaving."

"Sir..." He hesitated. "I debated breaking it off, to be honest. I don't like leaving her behind to worry. Don't like putting her through that." He ran his hand through his hair. "I'm still not sure I shouldn't break it off."

He'd admitted that with a calculated risk. He knew full well that her father might be angry hearing such a thing. But that one little sentence would pave the way when he *did* leave. She could use that as an excuse for the break-up. It was genius.

So why did he feel as if he wanted to throw up after saying it?

"I think you underestimate Kayla. She can handle it." He finally looked away from his daughter and turned those blue eyes that were so like Kayla's on Cooper. "If she loves you, she'll be fine. I was a cop while she was growing up, and always in danger. She's used to it. As far as partners go, she might be your best bet. She knows what she's getting herself into."

Cooper swallowed hard. He was almost tempted to agree with the man. To say fuck it, and ask Kayla to wait for him. But that wouldn't be best for her—it would be best for *him*. He refused to be selfish when it came to Kayla. She deserved so much more than an internet boyfriend.

"I'm sure she's perfectly capable of handling the stress,

sir," Cooper managed to say. "But still, I worry about her. I can't help it."

Her father nodded. Mr. Moriarity seemed to like this side of Cooper, which was ironic since it was the first time he'd been completely honest with the man. "I know the feeling. I've been worrying about her since the moment I first laid eyes on her. She thinks we're old-fashioned because we want to see her settled down. But that's not it. I just want to know that if something happened to me, she'd be okay, you know? That someone would take care of her."

Cooper finished his drink. He knew what her father wanted from him—a promise that he would watch out for his little girl. The problem was, he couldn't give it.

He'd made up his mind. He was leaving on Tuesday and he'd never see Kayla again. A fake relationship was one thing. A real one… Too complicated.

"I get that, sir." He stood up and lifted his empty glass. "But for now, I need another drink. I'll talk to you soon."

"Son?"

Cooper stiffened. "Yes, sir?"

"Just be good to her. That's all I ask."

Cooper nodded and walked away. Damn it all to hell, this was getting too serious and too damn *real*. Her father was asking him to take care of her, and he *wanted* to.

He really fucking wanted to.

Chapter Seventeen

Kayla leaned back against the car seat and watched the hotel grow closer and closer. They were almost back, and all she wanted to do was rip off Cooper's clothes the second they walked into their room. The time was ticking away over their heads, and she knew he felt it, too.

He'd been quiet. Really quiet.

They parked in the lot, but Cooper didn't move. She eyed him, trying to decide how best to proceed. "Did my dad break you? I knew I shouldn't have let you talk to him alone."

He looked at her, as if surprised by her question, then smiled. It looked forced. "No, he was on his best behavior. We just talked about deploying and expectations."

"I see." She opened the car door. "You ready to go up and have some real sex in our fake relationship?"

He unbuckled. "Is that really a question?" he teased, but it sounded hollow.

"You tell me, quarterback."

He opened his door, climbed out, and closed it behind him. By the time she had one foot on the asphalt, he was there. He wrapped an arm around her waist and then closed her door for her. "When it comes to you, I'm pretty much always ready."

"Sounds promising." She curled her arms around him, resting her hand right above his hip. "I feel the same way, just so you know."

"Good to know."

They pushed through the front entrance, and then made their way to the elevator in silence. By the time they reached their floor, Kayla knew Cooper's distant behavior wasn't all in her head. He was tense and silent. The only question was…why?

There was a fifty-fifty chance he was upset because their time was almost up. She knew she was—and she also knew she was willing to turn this fake relationship into a real one. It was scary and exhilarating all at once. The odds were stacked against them.

But she was willing to try, if he was.

He closed the room door behind him and leaned against it. After releasing a deep breath, he met her eyes. "Kayla…" His shoulder muscles bunched and flexed as he dragged his hands down his face. "We need to talk."

He'd been completely relaxed all those times he'd said he didn't want a relationship. So if he was *this* nervous about talking to her it must mean…

Oh God. This was it. He was going to ask to see her again after the wedding.

This was the first time she didn't want to run in the

opposite direction at the thought of a guy uttering those words, and it was thrilling. She'd let him speak first. Maybe he even had some big romantic speech planned, like in the movies—Cooper was good with the big gestures like that. She tried to calm her racing heart and sound casual. "Sure. What's up?"

"This whole thing between us...it moved really fast." He pushed off the door and crossed the room until he stood directly in front of her. "We met in an airport, and before the plane landed, I already knew the little sounds you make when you come. Ever since, it's been a whirlwind of craziness. I think we need to take a step back and reevaluate our plan. I think we need to talk—as much as I hate talking about this shit."

"I think I know what you're trying to say, and I agree wholeheartedly." She grabbed his hands and squeezed them reassuringly. "I'm not going to lie. It's been on my mind a lot, too."

He blinked at her. "It has?"

"Yep." She smiled at him. "I never thought I'd say this in a million years, but here I go. I...I..."

She couldn't finish. She could feel herself chickening out.

"You can say it." His voice was hollow, but he didn't seem upset, by any means. He seemed...relieved. "I've been thinking it, too, so it's a huge relief. You want me to leave, and I think that's for the best."

And just like that, the world crashed around her.

"Wait. What?" She dropped his hands, shock ricocheting through her body. "That's *not* what I was going to say. You want to leave? Why?"

"What do you mean *why?* I thought that's what you were

going to say. You said you were thinking the same thing as me…" Then his eyes went wide. "But you obviously weren't. What were *you* thinking?"

"Well…" She hesitated. Should she really confess her feelings after he admitted he wanted to leave, for the love of God?

But it was Cooper…

He shifted on his feet. "It can't be that bad. Just tell me."

She took a deep breath. There was nothing to be afraid of. The worst case scenario? He said no. She'd be fine. The rejection wouldn't break her. "All right…I wanted to keep in touch with you after this weekend. I wanted…more."

She saw his body tense. "What do you mean, keep in touch? You mean as friends?"

"Well, no, not exactly. I mean, maybe at first." She fumbled over her words. "But I'd like to be…more. Maybe? I don't know. We could text or email or Face Time. I mean, I know there's an eighty perfect chance of failure, but if we both worked hard at it—"

"You're babbling again," he said, his voice flat. "I don't understand what you're asking for."

"I know. I'm making a mess of this." She covered her face with her hands. "Forget it. Forget I said anything."

"It's too late for that." She heard him pick something up off of the floor and set it on the bed. Kayla lowered her hands and looked at him. But then she wished she hadn't. It was his suitcase. "You really want more than what we agreed upon?" He sounded as if he couldn't believe it.

"I do." She wrapped her arms around herself. "But something tells me that you don't. Am I right?"

He laughed harshly. "You're right." Suddenly, he looked

different. He looked...*cold*. "I thought we were perfectly clear on where we stood from the first day. Jesus, Kayla, I'm leaving the country in a couple of days. Why the fuck would you want to start a relationship now, of all times?"

"I know you're leaving. I'm not an idiot." She clung to her forearms so tightly it hurt. "And I don't know what you make me feel. I just know that I feel *something*. I like you a lot. And I'd like to know you even better."

Cooper opened the top of his carry-on. "You know how we said this was temporary, and that I could leave at any time if I changed my mind?"

"Yeah. Of course. You want to leave early?" She thought she might throw up at the thought.

"I don't, but I'm going to anyway." He was staring at her, but he wasn't really *looking* at her. It was as if she wasn't even there. "I'm not going to the wedding with you, and I'm not going to any more parties. It's over. We're done."

She froze, her heart twisting. "Is it because I want more?"

"Yes." He threw a shirt in his suitcase. "I told you that I didn't want a relationship. I told you why. Nothing has changed. I don't want you to fall for me, and I'm not going to fall for you. I have obligations, and they don't involve falling in love with a girl I met on a plane."

She stumbled back from him, trying not to feel betrayed. They'd both known going into this that they were temporary. That the relationship wasn't real. But he'd said he was going to stay until the wedding, and now he was running. Running from her, even though he'd promised to play the part until the wedding.

She'd thought he meant it. She'd thought she *mattered*. That had been her first mistake. Her second had been falling for him.

But he didn't need to know how deep her feelings for him were. They could part ways without him ever realizing the truth. "Then go. I'm not stopping you."

He dragged a hand through his hair. "Don't be like that. I'm doing this for you."

"For me?" She laughed. "Yeah. Okay."

He flinched. "It's true. It wouldn't be right to start something when I leave. For me to hold you to a promise when I'm going to be gone—and maybe even dead. You don't know what that does to a person. I do. I've seen it. You don't want it, Kayla. And you don't want me. Trust me."

"Oh, so the *man* says I don't want to worry, huh?" She held her arms out, finally, blessedly, pissed off. He was making decisions for her. Screw that. And screw him. "Well, if the *man* says so, then it must be true."

He slammed the lid to his case shut and zipped it up. "Don't turn this into something it isn't. I'm not fighting with you about this."

"Of course you're not. You already had the argument in your head and ended it before I could say a word." She gave him what she hoped was a feral smile. "You made the decision for me—what is there to fight about?"

He yanked his suitcase off the bed. "You weren't there, damn it."

"For our argument? You're right. I wasn't." She pointed to the door. "Now get the hell out. I thought you were different. I'm sad to say I was wrong."

He took a step toward her, his hand raised toward her. "Kayla—"

"No. Don't." She shook her head and backed up. "Just

go. We've both said enough."

She was such an idiot. She'd gotten attached to a guy who had told her from the start he was leaving. He'd said, point blank, that there wasn't a chance that this fake relationship would go anywhere.

And like a damn fool, she hadn't believed him.

• • •

Cooper watched her, trying to find the right words to make her understand he was doing this to save her from unnecessary pain. It was the hardest thing he'd ever had to do but he was walking away. She would be better off.

And then he could go overseas and focus solely on the job at hand. The job he was committed to doing with no distractions.

So why did he feel so…empty?

"That's not what I meant," he said. "You weren't there when my best friend died in my arms. You didn't hold him when he drew his last breath. And you sure as fuck weren't there to hold his fiancée as she fell apart piece by piece, either. But I was."

She sank onto the bed, perching on the edge. He finally had her attention. She looked as if she wanted to cry instead of throttle him to death. Not a huge improvement, but it was something. For some reason, it was important to him that she understood why he had to end things between them. She needed to get it, damn it.

"I'm not her," she murmured.

"I know you're not."

"And you're not him."

"I might be after I get back over there."

He half expected for her to point out that he didn't have to go, that he could stay, backed up with one of her kooky statistics. He was surprised when she didn't. "I can handle that risk. It doesn't mean you have to shove me away. Not if you don't want to."

"Kayla…"

"It's true that it'll be hard," she said, wringing her hands. "The odds are against us, yes. But if we worked at it and tried to make this real, we could—"

"Be the one in five *'dead and don't know it yet'* relationships that survive?" He pulled the handle out of the suitcase and squared his shoulders. "You know that we won't make it. You told me so earlier in this fake relationship. You're just in denial."

She made an angry sound, but she didn't bother to fight him. How could she? They were her own numbers he'd thrown at her. "You're not being fair. We don't know that we wouldn't have worked."

"You're right. And maybe that will haunt me for the rest of my fucking life, but I'm okay with that." He set his case in front of the door and then looked at Kayla for what would probably be the last time. Just the thought of it hurt. "You want to know why I'm okay with that? Because I watched Josh die, and then I watched his fiancée die with him. Hell, I even saw a huge part of myself die. I won't fucking do that to you."

"Just stop. Leave," Kayla whispered, squeezing her eyes shut. "Nothing I say will change your mind. So go."

"You could ask me to stay," he said, his voice raw. "Why *haven't* you asked me to stay?"

"Because that's not what you need. You need to go, and I understand that about you." She lifted her chin and looked him squarely in the eye. "I'd just hoped you would understand *me* better than you do. I wish you'd realize that I know my own mind and I speak my own truth. If I said I would be fine waiting for you to come home, it's because I meant it."

He crossed the room and pulled her to her feet. He expected her to fight him. To shove him away. But she didn't. Instead, she looked up at him with tears in her eyes. Fucking tears. "Don't cry. I never wanted to hurt you."

"I know." She gripped his forearms. "You wanted to help me. You always want to help people, and I was one of them. I get it. And I'll get over anything that I'm now feeling."

He wanted to tell her how much she'd come to mean to him in such a short time, but he couldn't do it. Instead he brushed his lips across hers, then dropped his hold on her. "I'm so sorry." He grabbed his bag. "Goodbye, Kayla."

"Goodbye, Cooper." She curled her hands into her jacket sleeves. She hadn't even taken it off yet. Hell, neither had he. "I hope you find what you're looking for."

He left the room and, when he reached the rental, he tossed his suitcase in the back. Then he slipped into the driver's seat of the Escalade, slid the car into reverse, and glanced over his shoulder at the backseat.

All he could think about was the first time he and Kayla made love there, after their flight to North Carolina. He could practically feel her skin on his. Her soft laughter teased his brain, echoing through the empty car and reminding him of what could have been, if he only stopped running.

But he couldn't. Not yet.

What the fuck was wrong with him? Why couldn't he just be a normal fucking guy for once? Live a normal fucking life with an incredible woman?

He slammed his fist into the wheel. "Son of a bitch."

This wasn't supposed to happen. He wasn't supposed to feel so empty at losing her. Hell, had he even really *had* her? Up until tonight, it had all been fun and games. Make believe.

Or had he been fooling himself all along about it being fake?

Taking a deep breath, he dropped his forehead onto the steering wheel and lowered his shaking hands to his lap. Rage, sadness, and frustration flew through his veins at breakneck speed, even though he knew he'd done the right thing.

He had to cut ties with her. It was better this way.

It had to be.

Chapter Eighteen

An hour later, Cooper pulled up in front of his hotel and got out of his Escalade. Kayla's words had played on repeat in his brain the whole drive, making him wonder if he'd just made the biggest mistake of his life in walking away from her.

Oh, who was he kidding? There was no wondering about it.

He'd made a *huge* fucking mistake.

But, hell, she'd caught him off-guard when she'd mentioned wanting more from him. Part of him had been elated, and the other part had been more fucking terrified than the time he'd faced down an entire band of insurgents with nothing but his rifle and lived to tell about it. The *last* thing he'd expected from her was her wanting more.

The terrified portion inside of him had obviously won out, and he'd taken full advantage of his fight or flight response by choosing the latter option. It was better this way. He knew it. But she'd looked so broken-hearted.

And damn it, he was, too.

If things had worked out according to their plan, he should have walked away from her feeling sexually satisfied and ready to move on to the next chapter of his life. He should be rejuvenated and ready to go overseas again, knowing that this time, he wouldn't miss the enemy hiding in the shadows. This time, he wouldn't fail.

But instead…he felt like utter shit.

After checking in and trudging to his room, Cooper sat on the edge of bed, yanked his collar loose, and flung his coat on the chair by the window. It wasn't supposed to be like this. He wasn't supposed to miss her already. Though he wasn't experienced in matters of the heart, he had a sinking suspicion he knew what the aching emptiness inside of him meant.

He wanted more, too.

Reaching into his pocket, he pulled out his cell. He stared at it, spinning it in his fingers as he debated his next move. He couldn't be impetuous. He had to think things through. Examine all the puzzle pieces before trying to make them all fit. He already knew he couldn't start something with Kayla and then leave. But there was one option he could take. One where he could be with her and this aching pain would go away.

It was time to call his dad.

His phone felt even heavier than the weight he carried around with him. The one that had *dad* etched permanently into it. In the month leading up to his interview, his father hadn't wasted one day trying to shove that damn position down his throat. Every time Cooper mentioned the upcoming interview, his father left the room. He came up with excuses to not have to hear about the opportunity.

Cooper had been certain his father couldn't stand being in the same room because he was disappointed in him for not staying in the Marines. That he couldn't stand being around his failure of a son. The same son who'd let his best friend die.

But maybe that hadn't been the case? Maybe he'd just wanted Cooper to take on his "life's work," as Kayla had called it. Maybe it was time they had a heart to heart.

He dialed before he could talk himself out of it, which would have been all too easy. On the second ring, someone picked up. "Hello?"

Cooper took a deep breath. "Hi, Mom. It's me."

"Hey!" A smile warmed up her voice. "How's North Carolina treating you?"

"Great. It's warmer down here, for sure."

"That's good." She paused. "Though, I guess you'll be a lot hotter soon. Over in the desert. I saw on the news it was over a hundred degrees yesterday."

"Well, yeah. It's definitely a lot hotter there." He scratched his head, wincing at the memories of the harsh, hot sun. The days he'd spent over there had been hell on Earth. "At night it cools off, though. Sometimes, it's frigid."

"But you're inside then right?"

He massaged his temple, picturing Kayla as she looked this morning, lying in bed and watching him with her bright blue eyes shining. He'd give anything to go back to that moment. Before all hell broke loose. Before he'd walked away. "Yeah, but it's not like I'm in a hotel or anything. It's mostly shoddy buildings and temporary housing."

"O…oh." She sniffed. "Well, you'll be safe, right? Promise me you'll keep safe."

She sounded so worried about him. For the first time, he felt guilty about that. He'd been so focused on making up for his wrongs, on proving that he could be the Marine he should have been when Josh had died, that he hadn't seen how it was affecting her.

How it was affecting *him*, too.

"Yeah, Mom. I promise." He hesitated, still wondering if this was the best course of action. Deep down, he knew the answer was a resounding *yes*. "Hey, is Dad around?"

He could practically see her pull the phone away and look at it, as if she doubted her hearing. The last time he'd "talked" with his father, it had ended in shouting and then dead silence. They hadn't talked since. "Yes, he's in his library going over ledgers."

In other words, he was sneaking a cigar behind his mother's back. It was a running joke, since it was common knowledge that his mom was fully aware of the cigars…but she humored his father anyway. How she managed to pull that off was beyond Cooper. The woman had a stronger sense of smell than a police dog on the scent and everyone knew it.

"Can I talk to him, please?"

"Of course." He heard her set something down, then open a door. She was probably walking from the living room, down the hallway, then down into his father's office. "Everything okay?"

"Yeah, I just need to talk to him." Cooper flopped back on the bed and flexed his arms over his head, stretching his muscles. "Need to straighten a few things out."

"All right. I'm almost there." His mom sighed. "But Cooper?"

He tensed. "Yeah?"

"Be gentle with him. It's always been his dream for you to run Shillings Agency when he retires, so finding out you had other plans hit him hard." She opened another door. That meant she was almost at the office. "I know he's been tough on you lately, but he doesn't mean to be. He's just… had to readjust his plans."

"I can see that, now. Being here…" He sat back up and bent over, resting his elbows on his thighs. "It's opened my eyes some. That's why it's time for us to talk again."

"*Really*?" She made an excited sound. "He's proud of you, you know. He's dying for you to take the reins—figuratively, of course—and that's all he's ever wanted."

"I know." He dragged a hand through his hair. "But Dad doesn't need to be handled with kid gloves, you know. He can hold his own in an argument."

"I know that all too well myself."

His mom knocked on the office door. He could hear her talking to his father, but it was muffled. Paper rustled, and a window opened. He barely made out something about "Cooper…" and "no cigars…" with a dash of "we'll talk *later*."

After another moment, the phone made a weird noise, and then, "Hello?"

His heart thumped hard. "Hey, Dad." What was it about his father's voice that always made him feel like an errant teenager? But tonight he sounded older. Tired, even. "How's it going?"

"It's going. I was in here sneaking a smoke, but Mom

caught me." He snorted. "It's the fifth time in as many weeks. She might skin me this time."

He grinned. "Sorry. That one was my fault."

His dad didn't say anything to that. "So, what's going on? I assume you're calling me at almost ten o'clock at night for a reason, and not just to chat?" He cleared his throat. "That isn't to say I don't appreciate the call. I do. I hate that we left things where we did."

Cooper stood up, his heart racing at what he was about to say. "There's something I need to know. Why do you want me to work with you so bad? When I left the military, I thought you'd be disappointed in me. That you wouldn't think I was fit for the company anymore. But then you kept suggesting it, and it started to feel the opposite." Cooper swallowed hard. "It was almost as if you didn't think I was qualified to get a job anywhere *else* anymore, so you kept insisting I just take the job with you."

His father grunted. "It might have felt that way, but I've never been disappointed in you over that. As a matter of fact, I've never been more proud of you than when you were man enough to admit the military wasn't for you. I just thought we would start fulfilling your duties at Shillings earlier than planned, but then you said no, and I didn't know what to do after that. I still don't know why you're against the idea of working with me."

Cooper widened his steps, pacing back and forth in the small hotel room. It was half the size of the one he'd stayed in with Kayla. He stopped walking, just the thought of her name making his chest hurt. "I wasn't against the idea, per se. I just wanted to earn the position. Get some experience in the field before stepping into the agency simply because we have the same last name. I don't like taking favors, Dad. If I take a job, it's because I deserve it. That's how it has to be."

"I respect that about you," his dad said. "I've been worried about you, son. Watching your best friend die…that changes a man."

When the familiar ache pierced his chest, Cooper closed his eyes. The pain had never fully left him since Josh's death. He didn't think it ever would. But for the first time ever, the pain wasn't paired with underlying guilt. Progress. "I'm fine. I'm not good yet, but I'm getting there."

"No one is *good* when they come home. Going to war can change a man. It can make you feel lost without a purpose to life. I know it did that to me." His father paused. "I was lost until I met your mother. Then I started working in private security. But until I had that… I didn't want you to come home and fall into the same destructive behavior I did. I didn't want to see you make the same mistakes as me, or get eaten alive by the survivor's guilt."

Cooper swallowed hard. "I'm not going to. Coming down here, it changed me. I'm not going to lie."

"Well, good. But you were already a strong man, son." His father's voice warmed. "I'm very proud of you, and proud of all you've accomplished. No matter what else you might question about me, don't ever doubt that again."

Emotion hit him in the chest, hard and mercilessly. He hadn't realized, until now, how badly he'd wanted to hear those words. To know, no matter what option he chose, that his father approved of him. "Thanks, Dad. I really…just, thanks."

"You're welcome," his dad said, his voice gruff. "You

keep safe over there, you hear? I'll be watching the news at the agency, making sure I don't see anything happening where you are, but still. Keep safe."

Cooper sank down on the bed again, clutching the phone so hard it hurt. Kayla had been right. And he'd been so horribly wrong to push her away. He didn't know if he could fix this mess he'd made with her, but he was going to try.

"So tell me…was it a girl?"

Cooper blinked. "W-What?"

"The change of heart." His father laughed. "Was it caused by a girl?"

"Yeah," he said with a chuckle. "It was."

"Your mother might have a heart attack when she finds out you met someone down there. She's been trying to find a nice girl up here for you, but something tells me she'll just be happy you finally found someone." A lighter flicked. His father was no doubt relighting his cigar. "Will we be meeting her when you come home from your assignment overseas?"

Cooper straightened his shoulders and tightened his fingers on his knee. It was time to go all in or nothing. If he wanted to be with Kayla, and he *did*, then this was the way it had to be.

All. Fucking. In.

"About that…"

Chapter Nineteen

This was it. This was the moment where the bride and groom would both say I do, and live happily ever after. Despite her own fake-boyfriend/real-heartache drama, she couldn't be happier for Susan and Max. Couldn't be more certain that they would be a statistic…a statistic for the marriages that lasted. They would conquer the odds.

They would live happily ever after.

As Kayla clutched the bouquet of flowers so hard her palms were sweating, Susan regally walked down the aisle, smiling up at Max with love shining in her eyes. Max looked as close to tears as Kayla felt.

God, she was going to cry.

This was one of the reasons she hated weddings. They turned everyone into a soppy, wet mess. She'd held it together when everyone asked where Cooper was. For a second, she debated lying and saying he'd been called away for work, but his boss stood right next to her. He'd know it for the lie it was, damn it. So she'd told them the truth.

She'd told them that they'd broken up.

Her father had been strangely silent through the chaos that had ensued. Her mother had scowled, disappointment clearly etched on her features, and Susan had sworn to rip his nuts off and feed them to the wolves. After way too many minutes, Kayla had shouted at the top of her lungs for them both to stop it. This was Susan's day. Not Kayla's.

And then the focus had gone back where it belonged — on Susan.

Her mom and sister were still angry at Cooper and she kept getting pitying glances thrown her way, but now that they were all in public, everyone was all smiles. Southern etiquette and all that crap. You could be pissed — but you had to be pissed with a smile on your face.

Up on the altar, Max tugged on his bowtie and grinned like a fool, filling the role of the lovesick groom to perfection. If Kayla were to describe the most heart-rendering expression on a groom's face she had ever seen in her whole life…it would be today.

Max really loved Susan. And he really was a great guy.

Cooper's face swam before her eyes — his startlingly green gaze, his rock-hard body, his sexier-than-sexy smile. Then she reminded herself he was gone, and she shoved the picture away. She needed to focus on Susan, not her own mess of a life.

Her sister had found happiness. True happiness.

How many people could say they'd done the same and not lost it?

"I take this woman, as my lawfully wedded husband —" Max cut himself off, his cheeks going bright red. "I mean wife. My lawfully wedded *wife*. I'm so nervous—I'm sorry."

Susan laughed up at Max, squeezing his hands. "It's okay. Take your time."

Max finished his vows without further issue, and when he finished he whispered three little words that only a few people could see—and Kayla was one of them.

He looked down at Susan and mouthed: *I love you.*

Kayla sniffed and wiped the tears off of her cheeks with the back of her hand, biting down on her quivering lip. Ah, hell. That was the last of her restraint.

Cue the messy tears. Except they were messy tears of happiness for her sister—a nice change to the river of sadness she'd cried last night over Cooper. But enough of that. Today was for her little sister. And Cooper could go back to the hell in which he was so determined to live.

Susan said her vows, then they exchanged rings and kissed. As Kayla held both bouquets, tears running down her face, she realized something. She *did* want this.

She wanted it with Cooper.

After posing for an obscene number of pictures, Kayla sank down into her chair at the reception hall and rubbed her sore jaw. Who would've thought smiling would cause so much pain? She relaxed against the back of the seat, taking a second to compose herself.

"Hey, sweetie," her father said, his voice coming from somewhere behind her. "Can we talk?"

Kayla peeked over her shoulder. "Hey, Dad. What's up?"

"I'm sorry Cooper left." He sat down. He looked older tonight, for some reason. Maybe because he'd just watched his baby girl get married. "I know you liked him."

"I know you didn't," she replied lightly. "But I'm fine. Today isn't about me."

"It might not be about you, but that doesn't mean I don't care." He sighed. "I want to see you settled down and happy."

He smoothed his tie and glanced over his shoulder. Susan was dancing with Max, and Kayla's mother was dancing with Uncle Frankie. Everyone looked joyful and carefree. She hoped to God she had done a good enough job appearing to feel the same way.

She picked up her glass of water and took a sip. "I appreciate that, Dad. But I've always been fine alone. I like being alone. I'm happy alone."

"Then why were you with Cooper?"

She could admit the truth. Say he'd been pretending to love her so that the focus would be on Susan instead of poor, single Kayla…but then Uncle Frankie would know Cooper had played them all. And that might affect him badly. Kayla wished things with Cooper could have been different—wished he'd been less afraid to take a chance on her—but she wasn't going to end his career because he chose to leave her.

She bit down on the side of her tongue. Cooper had told her she should just be honest and open, and that her parents would accept that. Maybe it was worth a try. She sighed and lifted her hands in submission. "With Cooper, I was different. He's the one guy I didn't mind giving up my freedom for. But the rest of the time? I prefer to be single. I don't want to settle down and get married. I don't want to pop out three kids before I'm thirty-five. I just want to live, and let life take me where it will."

Her father nodded. "I know."

"You do?"

Laughing warmly at her, he said, "Of course. Do you honestly think your parents don't know you at all?"

She felt her jaw drop. "Yes. I mean, no. I mean..."

"It's why you've been single most of your life, and it's why you moved to Maine." He shrugged. "You're independent. I think it's one of the things I admire most about you."

"Then why are you always trying to get me to settle down with a nice man?" She felt completely at a loss for words. "You're always pressuring me to get married. Always asking if there's a special guy in my life."

"That's because I was waiting for a guy like Cooper to sweep you off your feet." Her dad took a drink of water, then met her eyes. "I'm not going to live forever. I'm just looking for someone to take care of you when I'm gone."

"I can take care of myself, Dad." She reached out and squeezed his hand. "And you're not going anywhere. I forbid it."

He smiled, but it looked sad. "I would love to obey, but some things are out of my control. No one lives forever."

She swallowed past the lump in her throat. She didn't even want to *think* about that day. "I'll be fine, Dad."

He kissed her temple, then pulled back. "What happened with Cooper?"

"He broke up with me." She averted her gaze. "He's... he's leaving, and he didn't feel right leaving me to worry. He's scared that if something happens to him, I'll fall apart."

"He told me that last night. But I didn't think he'd break it off with you."

She sat up straighter. "Wait, he told you he was going to break up with me? Why would he tell you that?"

"Not in so many words, but he expressed his concern for you after he shipped out." Her dad rubbed his jaw. "I told him you could handle it, because I was trying to be supportive. But honestly? I think you're better off this way. I think he's right."

She stiffened. "I could have handled it."

"Yeah, you could have." He reached out and squeezed her shoulder. "But you deserve so much more."

"I'm so sick of people telling me they made the right choice for me." She curled her hands into fists. "I can make my own decisions."

"He's been scarred by his friend's death and the role he irrationally thinks he played in it. Not to mention the responsibility of watching over his friend's fiancée — a woman who, I'd bet anything, is struggling to adjust to life without her fiancé. He doesn't want to put you through the same thing. Is that such a bad reason to end things?"

"Not letting me decide for myself? Yeah." She lifted a shoulder. "But the motives behind them? No."

"Sometimes the worst actions come for all the right reasons, no matter how wrong they might feel." He finished off his drink and then set it down. "Do you understand my motives for being concerned about your welfare?"

"I get where you're coming from, yes."

Her father nodded. "Just remember that he and I aren't that different."

She tilted her head. "Are you serious?"

"Yes. He's scared you'll be hurt if he leaves." Her father stood. "And I fear the same. Not so different after all."

He left before she could reply. And honestly, she didn't know what she would say anyway. He'd kind of blown her mind. When he put it that way, she saw everything—her family, Cooper, her own life—in a whole new light.

She stood up and smiled at her sister, who approached with a dreamy look in her eyes. "Hey, sis."

"Hey." Susan hugged her. "I have a surprise for you."

"For me?" Kayla squinted at her. "It's your wedding, not mine. You're not supposed to surprise me."

Susan peeked over her shoulder, her whole body vibrating with excitement. "I know. But this one is a good one. Trust me on this."

"Oh, God. You're not going to try to marry me off to one of the groomsmen, are you?"

"Would you go for it?"

Kayla scowled in response, causing Susan to burst out laughing. "I didn't think so. Look, sis, I know you don't want what I have, and I know you're happy. We picked different paths, and that's okay."

"O…kay." Kayla studied Susan. "Where the heck is all this coming from? How much did you drink?"

"Enough." Susan giggled and grabbed Kayla's hand with a surprisingly strong grip. "Come this way."

Susan practically tugged Kayla across the room. And like a good Southern lady, Kayla kept the smile on her face, as if it wasn't weird that her bride sister was dragging her across the freaking reception hall or anything.

When they reached the men's bathroom, just outside the hall, Kayla dug in her heels. "Why are you taking me in *there*? I assure you I've seen one before—it isn't pretty."

Susan laughed. "Don't worry. You're not going in there. You're stopping right here. Just stand still."

And then Susan was gone.

Kayla scanned the room around her. The bathroom was to the left, and to the right was a sitting room of sorts. Gold couches, potted plants, dark wood tables and a mirror completed the décor. Oh. And *Cooper*.

Cooper was there, too.

"What are you doing here?" she asked, taking a step toward him and then stopping. "Why did you come?"

He gave her a tentative smile. "Can you come in?"

God, she'd missed him. "No. I'm staying here."

"Fine. I'll come to you." He reached her side, but stopped a few steps away. "I missed you."

"It's been a day." She wrapped her arms around herself. "It's hardly long enough to miss someone you barely know." *But it was.*

"You think I don't know you?" He raised a brow. "I think I know you better than anyone else in that room. They might know the 'you' that you show them. But they don't know the real you. Not like I do."

She shook her head. "It doesn't matter. You're not supposed to be here. We were done, remember?"

"What if I changed my mind?" His eyes locked on hers, green and irresistible. "What if I'm here to tell you I want to be with you?"

Then she would be speechless. But after talking to her father, ironically enough, she understood where Cooper came from with his determination to cut ties with her. And she didn't want him worrying about her worrying about him.

And she surely didn't need him making all of her decisions for her. "What if I changed my mind, too?" she said, her voice coming out as little more than a whisper.

"You're angry at me."

"I'm not anymore. I was." She pursed her lips. "But I get it now. You have noble intentions, and I do, too. You deserve to leave without having me dragging you down. You have a job to do…and I have a wedding to enjoy. So if you'll excuse me?"

"Wait!" He stumbled forward and tried to grab her hand, but she backed out of his reach. "I want to—"

"Kayla, are you okay?" her mom asked, coming up behind her and hovering like an anxious mother hen. "Why are you here?"

Cooper flinched. "I needed to talk to her. I got Susan's permission first."

"Well, you don't have mine." Her mom crossed her arms. "You can take yourself right on out—"

"*Mom*." Kayla shooed her away. "I'm fine. Just let him talk to me, and you go have fun. I can handle myself."

"Fine." Her mom's eyes narrowed on Cooper. "But I'll be watching you."

Cooper nodded. "I know."

When they were alone again, Cooper heaved a sigh. "Where were we? Oh, right. I was about to tell you—"

"It doesn't matter what you were going to say." Her heart twisted. "We're done."

He held a hand out. "Please. Don't say that. I'll stay for you. I *want* to stay for you."

"Stay?"

Her breath slammed out of her chest. He would give up his job for her? That was exhilarating, wonderful…and horrible, all at the same time. Because she wanted to say yes so damn badly. Wanted to be selfish and let him stay.

But it's not what he wanted. He'd been pretty damn

clear about that.

And what about next time his demons over losing Josh reared their heads?

"Is everything okay over here?" her father asked.

Kayla closed her eyes and counted to three in her head. By the time she hit three, she was ready to talk again. She opened her eyes and then managed a smile. "Yes, Dad, everything is fine. We're just talking."

Her father scowled at Cooper. "I'll let you talk, but I'll be—"

"Watching him," Kayla finished dryly. The moment was so frustrating she couldn't help but shake her head. "Yeah. We got it."

Cooper choked on a laugh, but covered his mouth to hide it. "I won't be long, Mr. Moriarity."

Her dad nodded. "Good."

Then he left, too. Cooper grabbed her hands and squeezed them tight. "I'm going to say this quickly in case someone else comes up. I'm fucking serious, Kayla. I want to stay with you."

She bit down hard on her lower lip. "Look Cooper, what we had was fun. Great, even. And I'll miss you, but you need to stick with Plan A. I won't be the one to take you away from it. Not in a million years."

"But I want to stay. You're not listening."

"No, *you're* not listening. I realized something today, watching Susan and Max. Watching my mom and dad, even. I do want a future with someone, a good one. And for a little while, I wanted that someone to be you. But I'm not going to compete with something that happened in the past. I'm sorry about Josh, about what his fiancée is going through.

I'm sorry that you feel responsible for it. But I'm right *here*, right *now*. And I think I've got a pretty damn good grasp of the things I can and can't handle."

He blanched. "Kayla, I'm sorry."

"I don't need your apologies." She lifted her chin. "And I'm not finished yet. I *can* handle someone not being here. I *can* handle the man I love being in danger. But what I *can't* handle is the fear that he's just going to run off whenever he decides it's best for me, regardless of my input. I want a partnership where I have a voice that's heard, even if the man in my life is halfway across the globe in a war zone when he hears it. So…there. Good luck with your job. I have to go back in now."

"I don't want your good wishes, damn it." He cupped her face, his grip firm yet gentle. His gaze clashed with hers. "I want you to believe me. I want you to let me be yours. And I want you to be mine. I just panicked for a second, and I pushed you away. I'm begging you not to do the same thing to me. Don't push me away."

"Kayla, is everything okay?" Uncle Frankie asked, his voice hesitant.

They both turned to him at the same time and shouted, "Yes!"

He stumbled back, blinking rapidly. "Okay, then."

And then they were alone again. Kayla covered her face and took a shaky breath. She couldn't do this. Couldn't do any of this. She wanted so badly to believe him, the same way she'd believed him when he promised he'd stand by her through the wedding. And then he'd bailed.

And now he was back.

And he was still holding her.

"Let me stay, Kayla. Give me another chance. Please."

She was tempted. So damn tempted. But could she trust him?

"I'm sorry, Cooper, but I need a man that will face his fears…not run from them. I can't do this. I can't be yours."

And then she left.

Chapter Twenty

Cooper watched her go, feeling more frustrated than ever before. He needed to find a way to get her to listen to him without interruption. If he could only get the words out without someone running to her side, breaking up their conversation, she might listen. Maybe then she would realize he didn't want or need the stupid job overseas anymore.

He knew that now, even if she didn't.

As he scanned the crowd, searching for her blue dress amidst the partygoers, desperation clawed its way over his chest, choking him. This was his last chance to prove he wanted to be with her and not in the fucking desert, and he couldn't mess it up.

Not this time.

When he finally spotted her, she was already halfway across the room. He would never make it to her side before she disappeared in the crowd, even if he shoved little kids out of his way to get there. "Kayla!" he whispered brokenly.

"You'll never catch up to her," Susan said, grabbing his elbow and dragging him in the opposite direction of Kayla. "Sorry, I was listening. What you said was great, but you need more power of persuasion—and you need it fast. Get on the stage and take the mic."

Cooper's heart stopped. And his stomach roiled. "I…I c-can't."

"Sure you can. I don't mind." She shoved him toward the stairs. "Go get her."

"I…I…" He racked his brain for another option—any other option—or for another way to get her attention before he lost her again. "Shit. I can just chase her down."

"No. It has to be a grand gesture if you want her to swoon." Susan shoved him again. Christ, the girl was stronger than she looked. "Haven't you ever watched a romantic drama? There *has* to be a grand gesture."

Grand gesture his ass.

He hadn't realized he'd muttered the words. Undaunted, the determined bride said, "Look, ditching my sister the night before my wedding was a shitty thing to do. So, yeah, you're going to have to counter with something just as big— except this time in a good way—if you want to win her over. A grand freaking gesture."

She had a point.

But Cooper feared the only gesture Kayla would get from him going up on that stage would be of him fainting like a fucking pansy in front of everyone in this room. But if that's what it took, then he had to find a way to give it to her.

His gaze fell to the microphone on the stage, and he swallowed hard. Could he get the nerve to go up there? To give her a sign he wasn't fucking around? That he was here to stay?

Hell yeah, he could. And he would.

His heart racing, he climbed the steps two at a time, not allowing himself to dwell on the fact that every single eye in the crowded room would be on him—that he was about to do the thing that terrified him most. Second only to losing Kayla.

He whispered a quick explanation in the DJ's ear, and the man looked at Susan for confirmation. At her nod, he killed the music and held the mic out to Cooper. "Go for it. Good luck, man."

Grabbing the mic with sweaty palms, it slipped out of his grip and clanged on the stage. A deafening boom filled the room and everyone grabbed their ears. As the crowd turned to see what caused the racket, he kept his focus on Kayla.

She hadn't turned around like everyone else. She was heading for the bar, her steps a little bit unsteady but obviously not from drinking. He could tell she was upset.

So was he.

Bending down, he grabbed the microphone with a firm grip, the other hand holding his knee for support. If he tried to stand up straight, he might pass out. "Kayla, d-don't take another step."

She stopped and spun on her heel, her eyes wide. "Get down from there," she called from across the room.

"Not until you listen to me."

"Cooper…" With a helpless expression on her face, she looked at Susan, but Susan just grinned at her—at least until the bride gestured for him to start talking.

Go on, Susan mouthed.

Shit. It was now or never.

He held the microphone in a death grip and forced himself to stand straight, despite the dizziness making his head spin. "You told me you wanted a man who would face his fears. Well, I'm doing it. I'm up here, ready to talk to you."

The whole room watched, frozen like elegant ice statues, no one daring to do so much as cough. Kayla walked toward him, her steps slow. "So talk, then."

"I'm going to start at the beginning and tell you the truth about that flight. I didn't have a first class ticket. I was supposed to sit in coach, but I paid an extra three hundred dollars to upgrade at the last minute after I met you."

She finally reached the floor directly in front of the stage. He tried to ignore everyone else. It was just the two of them—and he was not up on the stage. It was an old military trick of his. He needed to act as if nothing else existed but his target—and this time, his target wasn't the enemy. It was Kayla.

He took another deep breath. "I wanted to sit with you. I saw how nervous you were and knew you would be alone on the plane, with no one to help you forget about your fears. But it was more than that. I wanted an excuse to keep talking to you. I couldn't figure you out, and if I sat next to you on the trip…I would have hours to get to know more about you before we landed. I *needed* to know more."

She bit down on her lip and he couldn't tell what she was thinking. So he soldiered on.

"After I met you, I couldn't believe you were still single and sitting next to me. The first time I kissed you, I think I knew then that you were the one for me." He broke off and scanned the crowd, acutely aware of his captivated audience. After clearing his throat, he continued. "They say when you meet the woman you want to spend the rest of your life with, you know it. There's no questioning or second-guessing. You just know, like a punch to the face. That's how I felt about you. No, how I *feel* about you."

"Cooper..."

He held his free hand up. "When I met you, I told you I had to get this job overseas because I needed to make up for past mistakes. But you helped me realize that's not true. That this...this single minded determination I have to commit my life to righting an unfortunate accident isn't the best thing for me. You saw things in me that I didn't even see in myself. And that's something I love about us. We make each other stronger. Braver."

She smiled and blinked back tears.

"I know I don't need to be needed anymore. It's not a requirement for happiness. I don't need you to need me, but God I need you." He held his free hand over his heart. "I need you here. And I have you to thank for the new perspective I have on life." He looked out over the crowd. "All of you, actually. Thank you."

He focused again on her and only her again. She covered her mouth with her hand, as if struggling to maintain composure, and hugged herself with her other arm. It was time to finish this speech up so he could hold her. "When I left after our fight last night, instead of feeling ready to move on, I felt empty. By the time I got to the hotel, I knew I'd made a huge mistake. I knew what I had to do, and I started making phone calls. I started changing my life." He glanced at Mr. Holt, who was standing close to Kayla. "I'm not going overseas, Kayla. I'm staying in Maine, at my dad's company. And with you, I hope."

He saw her turn to Frankie, who nodded at her, an encouraging smile on his face. Turning back to Cooper, she took a step forward. Then another. Then another. "Cooper…"

He straightened his shoulders and waited to see if she'd accept him, flaws and all. "If you'll have me, there's a one hundred percent chance I'll be forever yours."

She grinned and put her hands on her hips. "So now you're into percentages, too?"

He grinned. "God yes. Those, and everything else that matters to you."

"Then there's a one hundred percent guarantee that I'll be forever yours, too."

"I thought nothing was one hundred percent in real life."

She held her arms out to her sides. "I was wrong."

"Thank God." He dropped the mic and leapt off the edge of the stage, his feet hitting the dance floor directly in front of Kayla. Picking her up in his arms, he spun her in a circle and then pressed his lips to hers. The crowd clapped and cheered.

He pulled back to grin down at her, wanting more than a chaste kiss, but it would have to wait until they had more privacy. Instead, he dropped his forehead to hers and hugged her tighter. "Can we get out of here before I puke all over the place? The aftermath of getting on stage is a bitch."

"Hell, yes." Grabbing him by the hand, she tugged him across the crowded room. They stopped in front of Susan and Max, who were both grinning from ear to ear. "Thanks for the use of the stage," Cooper said.

Susan hugged them both, laughing. "You're welcome. Now get."

Kayla winked. "Whatever the bride wants."

The second they cleared the restaurant and entered the lobby, Cooper stopped walking. He needed her *now*. "I want to stay here tonight. I'll go get a room."

"No need." She pointed over her shoulder. "I've got one already. I was planning on drowning my heartbreak with vodka cranberries and knew I wouldn't be driving since I don't have a car *to* drive. It's right down that hallway."

When she started walking again, he grabbed her hand. She shot him an impatient look and huffed. He smiled at her, cupping her cheek in his free hand. "I can't believe you agreed to a hundred percent."

She smiled. "We're a sure bet."

"I'm going to make you the happiest woman ever." He brushed his lips across hers. Light. Teasing. "Fair warning, though. I'm also going to make you fall in love with me. Consider yourself warned."

"Consider me scared." She ran her fingers down his jaw, her chest rising and falling rapidly. If he had it his way, he would do a lot more than make her breathe faster when they got to their room. "But honestly?"

He tugged her down the hallway. It was time to get her naked and screaming. "Yeah?"

"I'm already falling for you."

His heart skipped a beat, and he spun to face her. He backed her against the wall and kissed her, putting all of his feelings and joy in that one kiss. Still, it wasn't enough. Pulling back, he cupped her cheek and looked into her eyes, blown away by his happiness. "How did I get so damn lucky?"

She shot him a sexy come-hither look through her lashes. "I don't know, but you'll get even luckier once you get me into room 107."

"Well in that case, I'll speed up the process." He swung her into his arms, and she clung to his shoulders. "You were right, you know."

"About what?"

"My father. We talked it out last night."

"Oh yeah?"

"Yep. He isn't ashamed of me, and he isn't giving me the job because of my last name. He really thinks I'm the best. After the whole thing with Josh, I'd lost all faith in my abilities. He knew what was going on and was trying to reassure me that I still had the goods, but I was just too much of an ass to believe him."

"I *know* you're the best."

His heart sped up. "Thanks. And thanks for opening my eyes. I told him I'll train for a year, and then I'll consider taking over the company. I still believe I need to work my way through the ranks—and he agreed." He took a deep breath. "So I start at Shillings Agency next week."

"That's amazing." She offered him a sheepish smile. "I talked to my dad, too. You were right about my parents. They really do love me, and even understand me."

He laughed. "I know."

She swatted his shoulder. "No need to be so cocky."

"I can't help it. I'm a cocky bastard." He buried his face in her neck, inhaling her sweet scent. "And I'm selfish, too. I can't wait to get you home so I can keep you all to myself every single night."

"Oh God." Kayla groaned and dropped her head on his shoulder. "Thanks for reminding me that we have to fly home. Why'd you have to go and ruin my happy buzz?"

He chuckled. "Don't worry, I'll be with you. I have ways to keep your mind off the fear."

"Hm." She smoothed his suit jacket and entwined her hands behind his neck. Pulling him closer, she added, "And what ways are those?"

He opened the door and kicked it shut behind him. Backing her up against the wall, he tilted up her chin. He took a moment to savor her like this.

Passionate. Wanting. Beautiful.

He tugged up her thigh until she took the hint and wrapped her legs around his waist. Then he ran his hands down the curves of her body.

"Distraction…"

Epilogue

Kayla sat on the plastic chair in the airport, fidgeting with her purse and glowering at the waiting death trap she could see through the window. Christmas carols played in the background, and people laughed and chatted merrily.

Not a big shocker there. It *was* Christmas time.

And for the first time, she'd sent out a couples Christmas card. The same ones she always rolled her eyes at? Yeah. She'd done it. And she and Cooper had laughed at their matching red sweaters with every stamp they stuck on. She'd never had so much fun sending out cards, for the love of God.

But then again, she'd never had so much fun, period. He made her laugh every single day, and she constantly thanked God that he'd been stabbed in the stomach with a candy cane a year ago. She thanked God for *Cooper*.

Speaking of which…he was heading her way.

His green eyes were locked on hers, and he wore a smile, a grey sweater, and a pair of casual jeans. His hair was tousled to perfection, and he looked as if he was the happiest man on Earth. He always told her he was.

A kid with a candy cane ducked in front of him, and he lunged back. Kayla laughed, then covered it up with her hand. But he'd heard it. He turned to her with a mock glare. "You find my fear of kids with candy funny?"

"Um…we promised not to lie to each other. So I'm going to have to go with a *yes*."

"What are the odds of me being stabbed again?"

"I'd put it at one in a billion." She looked out the window, all traces of laughter fading away. "But our chances of crashing? Much higher. Like, one in—"

"Hey, now. None of that." He sat down beside her and threw his arm over her shoulder. Leaning down, he kissed her temple and then rested his cheek on top of her head. "We talked about this, and I'll be there the whole time to help you through it."

"We should have driven."

"To England?" He cocked a brow. "Even you know that's not possible."

That was her present from him. She'd told him she wanted to go almost a year ago—and he'd made it happen. He was so *perfect* it was almost sickening.

"When I said it was my dream to go to England at Christmas time, I didn't think it through." She fidgeted with her purse again. "Maybe we could take a cruise ship, or a submarine. Maybe before we die, they'll make a really, really long bridge. And then we can drive across it on the safe ground—"

"Over miles and miles of water," he said dryly.

"And not crash to our deaths." She peeked at the plane. "Oh God. We're boarding soon. Oh God."

"First class, you may now board," crackled over the speaker.

Cooper stood and held out his hand. "Ready, sweetheart?"

"No. Yes. I don't know." She took a shaky breath and then rose. "I'm scared. This is a long flight."

"It'll be fine." He led her toward the gate attendant. "Before you know it, we'll be drinking tea and eating biscuits with the queen."

She snort-laughed. "Or recovering from the massive hangover from the in-flight beverage service."

Kayla watched Cooper hand the gate attendant their tickets, then they walked down the jetway hand in hand. He held on to her so tightly that she wondered if he thought she'd try to run.

She was almost tempted to.

He stopped at the back row of first class and motioned her to her window seat. "Here we are."

"Okay. I can do this." She slid into the window seat. "I might be taking a sleeping pill for this one."

"You mean a 'vitamin'?"

She laughed. "Yeah."

"You can drool on me. Wouldn't be the first time."

She pulled the tray down and wiped it off with one of her ever-present anti-bacterial wipes, then handed Cooper one for his. He shook his head but did as she asked, then they both waited. She waited for this plane ride to be over and he waited for...*what*?

He looked nervous.

As they sat there, he tapped his foot on the floor and drummed his fingers on his knee at the same time. He was *fidgeting*. He never fidgeted. "You okay over there?"

"Huh?" He turned to her and blinked. "Oh. Yeah. Fabulous."

She pursed her lips. "Don't tell me you're nervous about this flight."

"Of course not," he scoffed. He craned his neck and looked over his shoulder. "I'm just waiting for our drinks. I ordered them before we even got on the plane."

She glanced out the window. "They'll be here. I think we're taking off soon."

"You need a drink before we do." He stood up. "I'll go and grab—"

"She's coming." Kayla grabbed his hand and yanked him back down into his seat. "And you're not leaving me. If you aren't here when we move, I'll lose it."

He patted her leg, but still seemed distracted. He was watching the flight attendant as if he knew her or something. "I'm not leaving," he assured.

The flight attendant came over and smiled at them. "Here is the champagne you requested, sir."

"Thank you." Cooper took the glasses, then handed one over to Kayla. "And if you have a blanket, that would be great."

"I can do even better than that. I could bring two."

"One will do." Cooper grinned. "We share."

The attendant nodded, while Kayla blushed. She knew exactly why he wanted that blanket—and she couldn't freaking wait. "It's a little more crowded in First Class than last time."

"Then you'll have to be even quieter." He turned to her

and held his glass out. Was it just her imagination, or did his hand tremble? "I love you."

"I love you, too." Kayla leaned in and kissed him, not bothering to take a drink. All she needed was right here with her. "Thank you for my present."

"Thank you for loving me." He lifted his cup. "Now drink."

She lifted it to her lips and took a sip. It was delicious.

He took a shaky breath. "I've never been happier than I have been with you, you know. I thought over all the ways I could do this, and a million scenarios came to mind. But the best one was staring me in the face." Cooper reached into his pocket. She arched a brow and watched. What was he up to? "Tell me, what are the statistics for people who get engaged? How many of them get married?"

Her glass hit the tray with a clunk. "W-What?"

"You heard me," he said softly. "What are the numbers?"

"I-I don't know." She wrung her hands in her lap. "Maybe Eighty? Why are you asking me this?"

"The chances you don't know the answer to that question are one in a hundred." He pulled a black box out of his pocket. When he opened it, she saw that it held a beautiful diamond. "Kayla, will you do me the honor of being my wife? I promise to spend the rest of my life making you as happy as I possibly can—distracting you on planes, and making you laugh—with a few fights thrown in for the amazing make-up sex. Will you say yes?"

She covered her mouth with her hand, then nodded frantically. "Yes! And not just temporarily yours. Forever yours."

Unable to stop himself, Cooper grinned and slid the ring onto her finger. "Fuck yeah. Let's do this."

Their laughter could be heard throughout the plane.

BONUS
Material

Keep reading for bonus content from the book!

Note from the Author

The scene you're about to read was originally between Chapter Twelve and Chapter Thirteen. In the first version, Kayla's mother calls up Cooper on stage. If you've already read the book, you know he has horrible stage fright, so this didn't work out so well for him.

Also, in the earlier version of this book, *Cooper* was the one who wanted to stay with Kayla at first, as opposed to the other way around. Kayla was against relationships, due to her knowledge of how often they failed, and he was kind of flopping around, trying to convince her to take a chance on him. She wasn't buying it at all.

Funny, how much a book changes with some tweaks. This scene doesn't fit with the characters anymore in any way, shape, or form — which is why I thought it would be fun to show you! You'll get to see how much Cooper and Kayla changed through the various editing stages, which I thought would be fun for us all.

Happy Reading!

Diane

Deleted Scene

One breath in, one breath out. Slow. Steady. Calm.

Cooper doubled over and took a deep breath of frigid air, his heart pounding a loud staccato in his ears. His blood pumped with rage, and he held on tight to his knees. Fuck, the last time he'd been so damn humiliated had been that Marine Corps Ball he'd told Kayla about earlier—and if he was as humiliated as that night? It was saying a lot. He hadn't thought anything could top that night.

When every single person in the restauranthad turned and stared at him as if he was some form of freak never before heard of, his whole body went tense. Then, to top it off, some of them laughed at him. They laughed, as if no one had ever heard of someone with stage fright, for Christ's sake.

It wasn't exactly an unprecedentedphenomenon.

Cocky fuckers.

But what in the world possessed Kayla's mother to call

him out like that? He was a virtual stranger to her...one that had no right speaking at an intimate family affair. No wonder Kayla made up boyfriends instead of bringing them home. Her family was one cluster-fuck of nosy, loud, rude people who couldn't mind their own business.

Then again, weren't all families in their own way?

The door opened and Kayla came stumbling out in her strapless, purple dress and black heels. Her breath puffed out in short bursts of steam as she made her way to his side, her pretty little lips in a worried pout. She grabbed his elbow, her delicate vanilla scent washing over him like the best sort of medicine. Stronger than morphine, and faster than anesthesia. "I'm so sorry, Cooper. I had no idea—"

"I know." He wrapped her in his arms and hugged Kayla close, more for her comfort than his. Unable to resist, Cooper buried his face in her hair. "It's okay. Don't worry about it. It's fine."

"No, it's not." She pulled back and looked up at him. The wrinkle on her forehead and the way she pressed her mouth shut tight showed him how earnest she was. "I had no idea she would do something like that. It was so nice of you to come to the bottom of the stage to meet me after my stupid speech."

Nice? He wasn't nice. He was certifiably fucked up.

How could she not see that?

"Your speech was perfect. I've never heard such a touching one before." He grabbed her chin and raised a brow. "Did you mean any of it? Do you really think your sister and her fiancé will be together forever?"

"I hope so." She licked her lips, and he watched the moisture spread over the pink flesh, but then she pressed them closed. "I mean, I guess they have a better shot at staying together than some people, but no one really stays married forever anymore."

"My parents are still happy—and I don't think that will change. If anything, they get happier every year. Or, so they say."

She shrugged. "Then they should thank their lucky stars."

For some reason, her cynicism bugged him. If she refused to believe that a relationship could work, despite the depth of love between two people, then he'd neverstand a chance in hell of making her want to be with him. Though they'd agreed to separate after the wedding, some part of him hoped she might want more at the end of their time together. Because, God help him, *he* did.

He wanted more.

He shook his head."Maybe it's less to do with luck, and more to do with love. And hard work. Happy marriages do exist."

She sighed and shoved her bangs aside. "You don't hear about them very often. I mean, it does happen occasionally, but not enough. Never enough. More than fifty percent of marriages fail. The odds are against love."

He dragged a hand through his hair and stepped back from her, his eyes on the darkening sky. Soon, the clouds would be hidden and the stars would be twinkling. He shoved his hands in his pockets and shivered. "For someone so damn hooked on statistics, when it comes to marriage and relationships working—you're fucking blind to reality."

She stiffened. "Well, excuse me. I didn't realize you were such an advocate for happily ever after."

"I'm not." He wasn't.

That was the kicker.

"Could've fooled me," she said, eyeing him with her nose scrunched up adorably. "I don't believe people have the dedication and love required to live together forever. Nothing will make me think otherwise. Not even statistics."

Should he spout off some fake statistic just to get to her? Probably not. He'd more than likely walk away with a stiletto sticking out of his chest if he did. Rubbing the spot where the imaginary shoe stuck out of him, he mumbled, "Think what you want. I'm not here to change you, or your opinions."

She nodded. "Good. Because I won't change."

"Good," he echoed.

They studied each other, neither speaking. Laughter sounded from inside, and she glanced over her shoulder. Wrapping her arms around herself, she turned back to him. "It's cold out here." She rubbed her palms across her arms and shivered. "You want to go back in?"

No, he didn't want to. He wanted to take her back to the hotel and pretend the rest of the world didn't exist. He sighed. "Yeah, but I need a drink."

"I think we both do," she said distractedly. "This fake-relationship stuff feels all too real sometimes, doesn't it? Did we just almost fight?"

"Almost." He opened the door for her, his stomach clenching when she brushed against his chest. There it was again. That never-ending need to have her. His fingers itched to grab her and pull her close. To kiss her until they both forgot about everything except this. "But we stopped, so it wasn't a *real* fight."

His eyes struggled to adjust from the afternoon sun to the dim interior lighting. Servers rushed from the kitchen to the seating area, and laughter filled the room. She glanced back at him, her soft hazel gaze torn in indecision. "Are you sure — ?"

He caught her wrist and pulled her closer, closing his arms around her. There she went again, questioning everything about them. About him. If she wouldn't listen to him when he said they were fine, maybe she'd believe him when he held her close. Touched her. Cherished her. "Yes. I'm fucking sure."

When her body melded to his in all the right places, she let out a gasp that made him grin in satisfaction. "*Cooper.*"

"I'm fine. Okay?" He dropped a kiss on her head, hugging her close for a brief second. If felt good."Now watch where you're going before you crash into something."

"I'm not that clumsy," she muttered, pushing away with red cheeks. "I'm going to have to introduce you to my dad in a minute, but we'll get our drinks first. I'll need some liquid fortification for that encounter anyway."

They settled in at the bar, ordered their drinks, and then he turned to her. She watched him with narrow eyes, but as soon as she saw him looking she glanced away, her cheeks flushing red.She tucked her hair behind her ear. "So Saturday is our last night together before you go back to defending our country."

"Yes." He failed to mention that he didn't want it to end yet, because saying so was pointless. He might as well leave now, for all the good his admission would do for either of them. "We knew our time together would be brief, though."

She nodded, but didn't look at him. "Of course. Still, time seemed to pass by fast," she said, glancing up at him, then quickly turning away, "didn't it?"

The drinks came, saving him from answering. There was nothing to say. He wasn't free to enjoy life. He had penance to pay. Penance for living when his best friend died. He didn't deserve her. Not yet. Though they might not have a lot of time left together, he could damn well make the most of what they had.

Leaning in, he pressed a soft kiss to her lips. It wasn't necessary for the ruse, but he couldn't fucking resist. She looked so damn kissable right then. "It really did."

She blinked up at him, her gaze darkening with passion. He loved her eyes. Loved the way they sparkled when she got excited. Or the expression on her face right before she came. He'd never forget her. Never forget this. When they got back to their room, he'd give her five minutes to be naked and waiting for him.

That's all the patience he had in him.

"Why are you looking at me like that?" she asked, breathless.

"Like what?"

She hesitated. "Like you're counting the minutes till we get back to the hotel room."

He placed a hand at her lower back, lowering his mouth to her ear. Dropping his voice to a whisper, he said, "Because I am. Time's almost up, and all I can think about it getting you alone, stripping off that dress, and making you call out my name so loud the bottom floor of the hotel hears it."

She glanced across the room, then back at him with a mischievous smile. He loved it when she looked at him that way. It usually meant she was up to no good. "Let's go say hi to my dad, finish our dinners, and then make a run for it. An hour tops. Deal?"

He chugged his whiskey. "Fuck yeah, it is."

"Then let's go," she said, hopping off the stool and picking up her still full drink.

He slid his hand into hers, and drew in a deep breath as she led him across the crowded restaurant. As she walked, she looked up at him with warm eyes and soft lips.

If anyone could save his damned soul, it would be her. If there was a way for him to come to terms with his shortcomings, he suspected it would be in her arms. But would it be enough?

Would *he* ever be enough?

Acknowledgments

Thank you, Shannon, for being a wonderful editor and always being in my corner. I appreciate you, and I'll miss having you by my side! Love ya!

Thank you to the whole Brazen team, for helping this book shine! The cover, the editors, all of you! Thank you so much!

To my family, I love you. Thank you for never letting me doubt myself, and for always being there for me.

To my agent, Louise, thank you for being my rock star agent. You're the best!

To all my friends and loved ones, thank you! I don't know what I'd do without you!

And, as always, a huge thank you to the readers out there. Without you, I wouldn't be doing what I love…

Writing sexy romance books.

About the Author

Diane Alberts is a multi-published, bestselling contemporary romance author with Entangled Publishing. She also writes *New York Times* and USA TODAY bestselling new adult books under the name Jen McLaughlin. Diane has always had a vivid imagination, but it wasn't until 2011 that she put her pen where her brain was and became a published author. She is represented by Louise Fury at The Bent Agency. Though she lives in the mountains of Northeast Pennsylvania with her four kids, a husband, a schnauzer mutt, a cat, and a Senegal parrot, she dreams of being surrounded by hot, sunny beaches with crystal clear water. In the rare moments when she's not writing, she can usually be found hunched over one knitting project or another.

www.dianealberts.com

Pick up the latest Brazen by Diane Alberts!

FALLING FOR THE GROOMSMAN
a *Wedding Dare* novel by Diane Alberts

Photojournalist Christine Forsythe is ready to tackle her naughty to-do list, and who better to tap for the job than a hot groomsman? But when she crashes into her best friend's older brother, her plans change. Tyler Dresco took her virginity during the best night of her life, then bolted. The insatiable heat between them has only grown stronger, but Christine wants revenge. Soon, she's caught in her own trap of seduction. And before the wedding is over, Tyler's not the only one wanting more…

More Entangled titles by Diane Alberts

TRY ME
Love Me

Play Me

Take Me

On One Condition

Divinely Ruined

Faking It

Kiss Me at Midnight

Made in the USA
Coppell, TX
27 March 2023

14838075R00125